SUMMER'S PATH

ALSO BY SCOTT BLUM

WAITING FOR AUTUMN

The above is available at your local bookstore,
or may be ordered by visiting **scottblum.net** or:

Hay House USA: **www.hayhouse.com**®
Hay House Australia: **www.hayhouse.com.au**
Hay House UK: **www.hayhouse.co.uk**
Hay House South Africa: **www.hayhouse.co.za**
Hay House India: **www.hayhouse.co.in**

SUMMER'S PATH

scott blum

HAY HOUSE, INC.
Carlsbad, California • New York City
London • Sydney • Johannesburg
Vancouver • Hong Kong • New Delhi

Published and distributed in the United States by: Hay House, Inc.:
www.hayhouse.com • *Published and distributed in Australia by:*
Hay House Australia Pty. Ltd.: www.hayhouse.com.au • *Published
and distributed in the United Kingdom by:* Hay House UK, Ltd.:
www.hayhouse.co.uk • *Published and distributed in the Republic
of South Africa by:* Hay House SA (Pty), Ltd.: www.hayhouse
.co.za • *Distributed in Canada by:* Raincoast: www.raincoast
.com • *Published in India by:* Hay House Publishers India: www
.hayhouse.co.in

Design: Amy Rose Grigoriou

Library of Congress Cataloging-in-Publication Data

Blum, Scott.
  Summer's path / Scott Blum. -- 1st printed ed.
    p. cm.
  ISBN 978-1-4019-2716-5 (hardcover : alk. paper) 1. Terminally
ill--Fiction. 2. Spirituality--Fiction. I. Title.

  PS3602.L864S86 2010
  813'.6--dc22

                                        2009038626

ISBN: 978-1-4019-2716-5

13 12 11 10   4 3 2 1
1st electronic edition, January 2009
1st hardcover edition, April 2010

PREFACE

The following story came to me shortly before the release of my first book, *Waiting for Autumn,* after that book had already been written. Because *Summer's Path* chronicles the three months prior to the setting of *Waiting for Autumn,* the decision was made to initially release it as a downloadable e-book before the first book came out in hardcover. And although the e-book touched many lives and I received several incredible letters from people who thanked me for sharing it, there was something that didn't sit right with me.

I didn't understand what bothered me at first— it just didn't feel finished. But I had already committed to releasing it before *Waiting for Autumn* came out, and I'm still glad that I did. However, with the benefit of seeing *Summer's Path* through the eyes of others, I was finally able to discover what was missing.

Even though the books are very different, the process of writing them was remarkably similar. They both came to me nearly complete in an instant as a download from the universe, and they both drew on many of my own personal experiences.

However, instead of having the benefit (or the burden) of my own life to communicate, as I did in *Waiting for Autumn,* I was tuning in to the lives of others in *Summer's Path.*

What I didn't realize while writing was precisely how we are connected to the people we're closest to. Of course I knew that we're all connected and are ultimately one and the same. But what I wasn't consciously aware of until later was that the connections that we forge with others are ultimately based on the common experiences we share. And when writing about others, the most profound insights come from those experiences that both the writer and the subject can relate to. It seems obvious in retrospect, but the way this manifested itself while writing the first version of *Summer's Path* was that I subconsciously contributed my own blind spots to others when telling their story. I didn't want to face certain difficult parts of myself while writing, so it was easier to leave them out altogether, and that's exactly what I did.

This book deals with some very difficult subjects that many of us will have to confront sometime in our lives. And through the writing process, I was fortunate enough to delve inward and reclaim several pieces of myself that I had successfully buried deeply for as long as I could remember. Thankfully I was given a second chance to retrieve some of the most sensitive pieces that had been missing, and it's a privilege to be able to share them in the two additional chapters near the end of this book that weren't included in the original e-book.

I believe that difficult experiences are gifts from the universe to help us on our journey. When we take the time to integrate *all* of our experiences with our present (not just the "positive" ones), we are able to draw from our entire past and ultimately begin to share our hard-earned wisdom with others.

And in that spirit, I am honored to share with you *Summer's Path*.

CHAPTER ONE

he pain in his abdomen was getting worse. It had been waking him up every night for the past week, and on this night he wasn't able to fall back asleep. He knew that he needed to rest, but sometimes walking around relieved the burning sensation that crept up at the base of his esophagus.

Don slowly pulled the covers back and quietly got out of bed, careful not to wake his sleeping wife. Suzanne was still working full-time as a bookkeeper for a small paper company while trying to take care of him. He felt guilty for what he was putting her through, and although he couldn't contribute financially, the least he could do was not wake her up in the middle of the night.

Making his way down the narrow hallway of their one-bedroom craftsman, he could see the full moon peeking through the open drapes. Their house was at the bottom of the foothills of town, but it was still up high enough that he could see the twinkling lights of Eugene that dotted central Oregon's Willamette Valley. It had taken them several years to save up for their first house, and it had been a badge of pride for them when they finally moved in.

However, Don couldn't shake the feeling that one day soon they might need to sell it and resume renting. He had been an engineer for a local semiconductor company since graduating from Oregon State University, but when a multinational had acquired the firm three years ago, it began to systematically "reduce redundancies" one department at a time. Unfortunately, Don's department was nearly decimated on a day eighteen months prior that he referred to as "Black Friday." He couldn't find another job in Eugene because his skill set was too specific, and when he got sick, he wasn't able to move to another city with a larger job market.

In the kitchen, Don caught sight of the microwave clock: 11:11. It was the third time in less than a week that he had casually glanced at a clock when it was that time. He wasn't superstitious, but the pattern was becoming regular enough to notice.

He began to look through cabinets and drawers for some antacid pills to help his stomach pain. In the back of his mind he knew they probably wouldn't do any good, but it was a habit and seemed to bring him emotional comfort even if there was no physical relief. When he opened the drawer containing the tarnished silverware that he and his wife only used during the holidays, he noticed a large stack of unopened bills from the hospital and various doctors he'd seen recently. He had been dreading this day ever since being admitted to the emergency room late one night, when the pain was so unbearable that he could hardly move. And although the hospital had to treat him, he couldn't forget the knowing look from the admitting nurse when he told her that he didn't have any insurance.

Don carefully removed the stack of bills from the silverware drawer and sat in the middle of the kitchen floor, fanning the envelopes around him in a semicircle. The envelope windows from the hospital bills revealed a rainbow of colors, starting with white, then progressing to more vibrant shades of yellow, orange, green, blue, and red. After they were sufficiently organized by color and size, he began to open the bills one at a time and glanced at the past-due amounts while placing them in front of him in two stacks—one for the emptied envelopes, and one for their contents.

At first he was calm, but as he opened more and more envelopes, he began to get angry. How could they charge this much for just a couple of days' worth of visits? And other than a few pain pills, they hadn't given him anything that helped. Most of the time was spent with doctors who didn't even know what was wrong with him, but they all charged full price even though they were absolutely clueless. And when they *finally* did figure out what was ailing him, they weren't sure how to deliver the diagnosis: "The good news is, we now know what's wrong with you . . ."

Being diagnosed with cancer at thirty-nine years old was one thing, but leaving Suzanne to pay off the hospital bills after he was gone hit him hard. The doctors couldn't agree on exactly how long he would live, but they all said that it wouldn't be more than six months. And although pancreatic cancer wasn't curable, the doctors presented many options that could be tried to temporarily improve the quality of life during his last few days.

But judging by the mountain of medical bills that Don had collected in the flurry of hospital and doctor visits during that initial two-week period, there was no way he could imagine spending any more of Suzanne's money just so he might die with slightly more comfort. The pain was excruciating at times, which was why he had gone to the emergency room that first night, but seeing how much money he had spent just finding out what was wrong temporarily numbed him.

Suzanne stumbled into the kitchen, rubbing her eyes. "What's the matter?" she asked. She looked down and saw the bills surrounding her redheaded soul mate. "Oh, you found those."

"Why didn't you tell me these came? Were you hiding them from me?"

"I wasn't hiding them. I just couldn't bear to open them. Is it bad?"

"It's devastating. It's obscene how much they charge. I counted twelve different doctors I didn't even see who billed me for things I can't even pronounce. If they're going to charge that type of money, they should at least have the decency to stop in and introduce themselves."

"They're probably not used to treating people without insurance," she said sadly. "We probably should've been married sooner." She nearly choked on the words as her eyes began to well up.

Don had proposed marriage to Suzanne more than a decade prior, but she hadn't been able to bring herself to marry him. Not that she wasn't fully committed, but she didn't want to let the government dictate what she considered to be a sacred agreement between two individuals. The fact that marriage was a state-sanctioned contract with financial incentives angered Suzanne to her core—love shouldn't be bought or sold. They had held a private commitment ceremony nearly five years ago, and in the end, even their families hadn't acknowledged their marriage because they weren't invited to the ceremony.

As the years progressed, their "statement" didn't seem to mean anything to anyone but them. Although that had initially been the point, it slowly began to make things more and more complicated, especially when it came to health insurance. The policy provided by Suzanne's employer didn't acknowledge domestic partners, so Don had remained uninsured since he'd been out of work.

Following the diagnosis, they finally went to the county courthouse and signed the papers to become officially married. But afterward they discovered that Suzanne's company's policy excluded a spouse's pre-existing conditions, so Don's cancer and related symptoms wouldn't be covered.

"In my mind we've been married for years," said Don. "We did it our way, and it was beautiful." He, too, was thinking about how much easier things would be if he had insurance, but he blamed himself for losing his job. He never regretted keeping their marriage private, although he couldn't forgive himself for being laid off. If he would have made himself more valuable, or if he wasn't so shy, he could have become friends with the new executives and might still have his job.

"But the insurance—" Suzanne couldn't stop her tears from flowing, and turned away from her husband as she silently cried.

Don crawled over to his wife and softly caressed her long brown hair. Seeing her break down made his heart hurt because of what he was putting her through. "I'm sorry," he said, the words barely audible as they caught in his throat. "I'm sorry for leaving you."

CHAPTER TWO

Over the next few weeks, Don's depression deepened. He seldom got out of bed, and he refused to eat more than a couple bites of bread a day. He found that the less he ate, the weaker he became. And the weaker he became, the more he would sleep, which gave him a temporary reprieve from the intensifying pain.

When he did emerge from bed, he would often gravitate toward the kitchen to open the silverware drawer. Every time he did, he would find more and more late notices piling up. They had nearly doubled in volume, and although there were very few entirely new bills, the late fees were quickly compounding, and the paper they were printed on became more vibrant in color. Additionally, the doctors' assistants began to leave answering-machine messages under the guise of concern: "The doctor would like to schedule a follow-up visit to discuss how you're feeling, but we need to take care of your outstanding invoice first. Please call as soon as possible, and we can work out a partial-payment plan if that's more convenient."

As his pain continued to worsen, Don began to research the costs associated with various treatment options. He knew it was a temporary fix, but the pain was becoming unbearable and he could barely function.

"I think it's time to go back to the doctor," Suzanne said one afternoon when she discovered her husband doubled over on the floor of the bathroom.

"There's nothing they can do," replied Don.

"They said that they could make you feel better."

"How? It's not exactly a curable disease."

"But they said that different treatments could make you more comfortable. Don't you think we should try chemo at least once to see if it helps?"

"Once isn't going to make any difference. Besides, do you know how much it costs? We still haven't paid a dime to those first doctors who didn't even know what they were doing. And the most expensive bill is the oncologist, who's the one we need to go back to for the chemo."

"We can start paying him a little every month so we can keep the treatments going."

"So we can go into even more debt? I don't think so."

Don had been researching how to pay for the chemotherapy treatments, and he couldn't figure out a way to make it work. He knew that they would probably let him start the treatments and perhaps allow him to continue until he succumbed to the disease. But the cost, even by the most conservative estimates, would burden Suzanne with financial hardship for many years to come. It was also likely that she would have to sell their house just to keep the collectors off her back for the first few years. And even that wouldn't be enough to take care of it all. He already knew that *he* had a life sentence—he wasn't going to impose another one on his wife, just because she had the unfortunate luck to fall in love with him.

"Some things are more important than money," Suzanne said softly. "I can't stand to see you in so much pain."

"Maybe I should just leave," he said. "Maybe my time is over."

"Don't even joke about that!"

Although Don had never said it out loud, it was something he had been thinking about for a while. When he first confronted his mortality after being diagnosed with cancer, he had to admit that he was afraid of dying and wanted to put it off as long as possible. He'd also made a promise to himself when he first met Suzanne that he would always take care of her financially, whether he was alive or not. Being able to do so after he was gone was his promise of immortality. And the thought that he would simply cease to exist, without leaving even a little bit of money to her, made him feel like his entire life had been a waste of time.

But the main reason Don didn't want to die was because he didn't want to leave Suzanne. His mother had died of cancer when he was only two years old, and his father had died of it when Don was a freshman in college. He had always felt abandoned by his parents, and he vowed that he would never be responsible for leaving anyone he loved, for any reason.

"Can I get you a pain pill?" Suzanne asked.

"They don't work anymore—keep them for yourself."

He didn't know how much longer he could tolerate the pain, but the thought of acquiring more medical bills felt even worse than his physical discomfort. Although the thought of ending his own life had initially repulsed him, it began to make more and more sense as a viable alternative. If he could work out the details to minimize the trauma inflicted on Suzanne, she might eventually forgive him and agree that it was the best solution for everyone.

Later that week, Don had an intensely vivid dream that felt incredibly real. It started in a light-filled tunnel swirling counterclockwise, with the path he was standing on remaining still. As he walked closer to the light, he saw his deceased father gesturing for him to go away. He was drawn closer in order to speak with him, but his father began to fade as he approached the spot where he'd been standing. Then the entire tunnel dimmed to blackness, and he could hear footsteps walking toward him.

As the ominous sounds grew more intense, he became acutely aware that he was standing completely naked. He felt vulnerable as he tried to cover himself with his hands. After several minutes, the footsteps were silenced and he could hear a figure breathing loudly immediately in front of him. As he tried to calm himself, he couldn't help but feel that there was something familiar about the sound of the breath.

Slowly, the figure came into focus as the light around them began to brighten. The man standing there was of medium build and dressed entirely in white. Don strained to make out the details of his face and then rubbed his eyes in disbelief. After his focus completely returned, there was no mistaking it—the person who was standing before him looked exactly like Don himself. It was a feeling similar to looking in the mirror, with two major exceptions: there was twice as much energy emanating from the reflection, and the figure's movements didn't correspond to his own.

Don's focus returned to the fact that he was standing there naked, and when he looked down, he was relieved to find that he was now fully clothed. He was wearing exactly the same outfit as the person in front of him, yet his own was completely black. He imagined that there was some significance to the fact that he was clothed in black while the other was in white, but he was just happy he was no longer naked.

There was a long silence while the two stood staring at each other, until Don finally said: "Hi."

"Hello," said the *other* in a voice that was nearly identical to Don's.

After another uncomfortable silence, Don finally asked the only question he could think of: "Who *are* you?"

Without pausing, the man answered, "I'm Robert—nice to meet you."

Robert stretched out his hand in a greeting, but Don just stood there looking at it, dumbfounded. Robert retracted his hand after a few seconds, and Don felt a smirk creep onto his face. The smirk widened into a full smile, and within seconds he began laughing hysterically. He continued to laugh for over a minute and then doubled over at the waist and slapped the ground next to his feet as tears streamed down from laughing so hard.

"Robert!" exclaimed Don in between chuckles. "That's classic! I finally meet my doppelgänger, and his name is Robert! Of course your name is Robert—why wouldn't it be?" He didn't know why the name struck him as funny, but it did. There was something ironic about a supernatural experience having such a common name.

"So, *Robert*"—he tried unsuccessfully to suppress his laughter—"what brings you here?"

"I'm here to help you." Robert was getting noticeably annoyed.

"Help me? Help me with what?"

"With your transition. Anything you don't understand or anything you could use some extra help with."

"My transition?" Don's laughter stopped instantly. "What transition?"

"Your transition to the next dimension—the next stage of your journey."

Don took a few moments to reflect on these words. "Are you the grim reaper or something?"

"Not exactly." It was now Robert's turn to laugh. "I'm more of an advocate. I'm here to help you transition in whichever way you choose."

"You mean you're here to help me die?"

"That's oversimplifying it a bit, but I guess you could say that."

Don felt a chill on the back of his neck. "Are you the angel of death?"

"I wouldn't say *the* angel of death, but I'm certainly one of them."

"You mean there are more than one?"

"Of course there are. Do you know how many people die every day? There wouldn't be time to do anything meaningful if there was only one of us."

"I have a question," said Don thoughtfully. "Why me? And—why now?"

"Everyone ultimately takes the same journey, and now is your time to be on Summer's Path:

> *Spring flowers wither*
> *Honey Moon condenses light*
> *Summer's Path begins."*

Robert smiled after reciting the haiku, and patiently awaited Don's response.

"Um, okay. I guess I've never really understood poetry," said Don. "What do you mean by 'Honey Moon condenses light'?"

"The Honey Moon is the first moon of summer —the moon that celebrates the summer solstice."

"Okay . . . but how does that *condense light?*"

"After the first day of summer, the days begin to shorten. Leading up to summer, the days grow longer, so it's easy to take light for granted. But as they get shorter, every second of light must be cherished."

"Is *light* a metaphor for something?"

"Light is our life force—the energy we need to exist. Whether you call it a metaphor is up to you," Robert laughed.

Don let Robert's curious words sink in before continuing. "It's ironic that it's called a *honeymoon,* like after a wedding. Don't you agree?"

"Not at all," replied Robert. "Actually, I can't think of a better word to mark the beginning of a life together."

Don sat down on the narrow path and put his head into his hands as he remembered *his* honeymoon with Suzanne at Crater Lake. He knew life was short, yet he couldn't help but feel he had been careless with his time with his wife. It saddened him to realize that he *had* taken his years with Suzanne for granted. And now it seemed as if he had once again come to a major crossroads. He needed to decide if he should let the cancer take its course or if he was prepared to shorten the process.

At that moment, the sound of a hundred voices began echoing inside his head. But the voice he kept hearing the loudest was Suzanne's: *"Don't even joke about that . . ."*

After the voices faded, Don slowly stood back up and looked deep into Robert's eyes, trying to decide if he could trust him, and if he actually *could* help with the transition. "Okay, you have my attention—what can you do to help?"

"I can start by giving you advice about how to make your transition easier."

"Like what?"

"The first thing you need to do is get your affairs in order. You don't want to unnecessarily burden your loved ones once you pass on."

"But I don't have any money."

"Yes, but you do have obligations, and that's even more important to figure out. I recommend you visit a lawyer immediately."

"A lawyer?" Don questioned. "Why do I need a lawyer? What should I ask?"

Robert had already turned and was walking away. He waved without looking back, and before fading into the distance, he said, "I'm an advocate, not a babysitter. Just go see a lawyer, and come back to me after you have the answer you need."

CHAPTER THREE

In the days following his dream, Don felt strangely disconnected from his body. He could see and hear everything that was going on around him, but it was as if his emotions had been packed into cotton and everything around him was happening in an adjacent room—almost as if he were watching a movie in a drive-in theater with the sound box turned down. He could tell that Suzanne knew something was up because she kept asking him if he was okay much more frequently than she used to. But in reality, Don hadn't felt any pain since meeting Robert, which was a welcome reprieve. And although he wasn't convinced that Robert was real, their conversation definitely made him think.

After nearly a week, Don was still wondering why he needed a lawyer. He tried to come up with different reasons, but it just didn't make any sense. Nobody was suing him, and *he* didn't want to sue anyone himself. He'd thought about suing the hospital and doctors for being so incompetent, but in reality they had eventually recommended an oncologist who *did* know what was going on. And realistically, the cancer had been brewing undiagnosed for quite some time, so there was probably nothing they could have done.

Then one morning as Don habitually shuffled through the late notices, he had an epiphany. What if a lawyer could figure out a way to get out of paying the hospital bills? If there was a way that he could clean up all the medical debts before he died, Suzanne wouldn't be burdened with paying them off.

He couldn't escape the feeling that Suzanne would feel crushed under the weight of the debt as the years progressed. The ridiculously high interest was already beginning to accrue, and with just the bills they had already received, Suzanne would be in serious debt for the next fifteen years. And the new bills kept coming—it seemed that every week there was another doctor who finally got around to sending an invoice.

Don began to get excited about the possibility that a lawyer could help make the debt go away, and immediately thought of his friend Eric whom he had gone to Oregon State with. They had both been in the engineering program, but Eric had decided he wanted to make more money, so he enrolled at an East Coast Ivy League school to become a lawyer when his undergraduate work was done. After graduating, he had returned to Eugene, where his well-off family had given him the seed money to start his own practice.

He and Don had gradually drifted apart, primarily because Eric had relentlessly hit on Suzanne once when he'd had too much to drink, and it made her very uncomfortable. Don told her that Eric treated everyone like that, but she was convinced that he had crossed the line, and didn't want anything to do with him ever again. Eric lacked an inherent tact, which made him a great lawyer but a less-than-ideal dinner guest.

Don found the phone book and dialed his friend's direct line.

"Eric, it's Don."

"Hey, bud, what's up? How's the sexy chica?" Eric always called Suzanne "the sexy chica," which didn't help her view of him.

"She's great. Are you still dating . . . what was her name?"

"Which one?" Eric laughed. "I don't remember who I told you about. I'm seeing a few sexy chicas myself. Chronic bachelor, I am."

Don attempted to join in Eric's laughter, but he couldn't. After several years of the same conversation, Don just felt sorry for him. "Hey, Eric, I have a professional question for you. Do you have time for a quick meeting?"

"I always have time for you, bud—let me see." Eric covered the phone with his hand and yelled something to his assistant. "You're in luck: my eleven o'clock just cancelled. But if you can't do it today, it's going to have to wait until next month. I'm going on safari for six weeks in Botswana. I'm leaving tomorrow. Gotta get back to nature, you know. It's going to be mind-blowing. Elephants and tigers and shit."

"Wow, Botswana. That's cool. But, yeah, I'd love to chat today at eleven o'clock."

"Okay, that's great." Eric put Don on speakerphone and began talking to someone else in his office. "See ya at eleven, bud."

Don got cleaned up and prepared to drive across town. He had never been fond of driving before his diagnosis, and although he still had his beloved Land Cruiser, he had seldom driven it since he lost his job. He was worried that the battery would be dead since the car had been sitting on the street for so long, but it started right up, and he made his way downtown.

Eric worked in one of the nicest buildings in Eugene—a large white stucco with an atrium in the center that was filled with natural light. After signing in with the security guard near the entrance, Don took an elevator to the top floor.

"I'm here to see Eric," he said to the receptionist who greeted him as soon as he entered the plush offices. Her imposing wood desk was perched in front of three large cherry-wood bookcases that contained an impressive collection of matching yellow-leather volumes.

"I will let Mr. Williams know that you're here. Please make yourself comfortable."

After several minutes, the receptionist led Don to Eric's office and gestured for him to enter. Eric was wrapping up another phone call and looked exactly the same, except that he had put on a few extra pounds. The added weight suited him nicely and gave him a physicality that finally seemed to match his personality.

"Hey, bud—great to see you." Eric walked around his large mahogany desk and stopped in his tracks, looking Don up and down. "You look like shit! What happened to you, bud? Are you okay?"

Eric's frankness always seemed to catch Don off guard. "Um, I guess that's part of what I want to talk to you about. Can we sit down?"

Eric gestured to a small leather couch in the corner of his office next to a floor-to-ceiling picture window. Looking out across Eugene, Don could see the neighborhood he lived in and tried to find his house.

As he sat down in the overstuffed couch, he noticed a small black digital clock resting on the end table. Don rubbed his eyes with his palms once the numbers came into focus: 11:11. He subconsciously held his breath until the last digits turned to *12*.

"Thanks so much for seeing me last minute . . . it really means a lot. But I have to let you know, I really can't afford—"

"Your money is no good here," Eric interrupted while waving his arms wildly. "You saved my ass in the dorm that day, and I'll never forget it."

Don remembered when Eric's parents un-expectedly arrived at his dorm one morning while Eric was still out partying from the night before. "Those were the days . . ." said Don.

Eric laughed. "So what's up?"

"Well"—Don sighed deeply—"first of all, I have cancer."

"Shit, man. Oh, shit. Shit, shit, shit. That totally sucks. Shit. Is it serious? What am I saying? Of course it's serious. Just look at you! Oh, shit. I'm so sorry, man. What kind?"

"Pancreatic."

"Oh, shit. That's what got your pops, right?"

Don nodded.

"They don't really know what to with that, do they?" Eric kept shaking his head. "What do your doctors say?"

"They give me anywhere between three and six months."

"I need a drink." Eric sighed loudly as he opened a discreet mahogany cabinet that was filled with a collection of whiskey bottles and crystal tumblers. "You?"

"No, thanks."

Eric poured himself a large glass and sat back down. "So what can I do? Anything, man. Anything."

"You know I got laid off at the semiconductor plant?"

"Uh-huh."

"Well, my insurance ran out about a year ago."

"That sucks. So you need money. How much is it?"

Don told him the amount of the medical bills so far.

"Wow, that's a lot. Okay, okay. Let me see. Yeah, I think I can do that."

"Thank you, but I'm not asking for money." Don knew Suzanne would flip out if she found out that Eric had paid off their medical bills. It was true that Eric hit on every female he met, but he really did scare Suzanne that night, and Don could imagine the possibility that his friend might use the money as a way of staying in her life after he was gone. He felt very protective of Suzanne as he repeated in a firm tone: "I'm not asking for money."

"It's no problem, really. What's money for, right?"

"Seriously, Eric, I won't accept your money. But I do need your expertise. Is there any way we can get out of paying the medical bills altogether?"

"Hmm, lemme think. Did they ask you to sign anything when you were admitted?"

Don nodded. "A bunch of things."

"Yeah, they wouldn't forget that—too much liability. If you want to bring by a copy of everything you signed, I'll look through it, but it seems like a long shot."

"Okay."

"The only way to get out of paying medical bills is to file for bankruptcy or to die." The filter between Eric's brain and his mouth didn't always work: "Sorry, man."

"No prob—"

"Wait," Eric interrupted. "That's it. You're dying, right? So that means the bills transfer to any legal heirs or assigns, and if there are none, they get written off by the company and go away!"

"I thought about that, but that means Suzanne would still have to pay them."

"Maybe not. You're still living in sin, right?"

"What?"

"You never got married."

"Yes, we got married—I told you that."

"I don't mean some bullshit commitment ceremony; I mean *really* married. Did you ever file papers with the courthouse?"

"Yes, we recently did that to get insurance—but it was too late."

"Pre-existing condition?"

"Yep."

"Well, you can get a divorce."

Don had already thought about that, also, but after waiting several years to finally wed Suzanne, there was no way he would intentionally taint their marriage just to save a few dollars. Their love was the most beautiful thing he'd experienced in this lifetime, and now that they were officially married, that was the way he was going to die.

"You can run up all the new bills you want," said Eric, "and Suzanne would only be stuck with the old ones. Go back to the doctors and get all the treatments you need. Get the best room they have. Tell them to spare no expense." Eric let out a loud belly laugh.

"I wish it was that easy," replied Don. "They've already made it perfectly clear that I need to start paying before I get any more treatments."

"You should go to my friend Dr. Bernstein. He's the best oncologist in Eugene."

"I did. That's who's harassing me for the money."

"Yeah, he's pretty shrewd," said Eric with a hint of admiration in his voice. "However, I'm sure he'll accept a partial payment. Let me pay enough to keep Bernie happy, and you can keep your treatments going."

Don shook his head.

"Okay," said Eric. "But let me know if you change your mind. The offer stands."

"Thank you."

"Sorry. I wish I had better news."

Although Don didn't like the answer, he was happy he had come. He now knew for certain that Suzanne would be responsible for all of the medical bills he incurred, which convinced him once and for all that he didn't want to do anything else that would add to the debt. "That's okay," said Don, feeling somewhat defeated. "It helps more than you know."

Don got up and shook his friend's hand before walking to the door. "Thanks again."

"Don't mention it. Let's get together when I get back from Botswana."

Don knew this was the last time he would ever see Eric, but he decided not to end the visit on a downer. "Absolutely," he said with as much enthusiasm as he could muster. "Enjoy your trip."

CHAPTER FOUR

"I was thinking . . ." Suzanne said softly while stroking her husband's hair. "What would you say to putting your seed on ice so we could have a child after you leave?"

Don burst out laughing. "My 'seed'? My *'seed'?!* Where did you get that from? Can't you even say the word?" It was the first time he had laughed out loud in a while, and it felt good. "What am I, a tree, now?"

His laughter was infectious, and Suzanne also let a smile emerge. "Okay, your *sperm,*" she laughed. "I would like to save some of your *sperm* so we can have a baby after this is all over."

Don's seriousness returned in an instant. "We've talked about having children before."

"I know—the world is a horrible place, and there are too many people in the world . . . blah, blah, blah. I just thought things were different now."

"Yes, things are *much* different now!" Don waved his arms to emphasize the point. "I'm about to die from a genetic disease, and there's no way I'm going to impose my defective genes on a baby!"

"They don't know for sure if it's hereditary."

"My *mother* died of cancer. My *father* died of cancer. My *grandfather* died of cancer. And now *I'm* going to die of cancer. How much more sure can you get?"

"I just thought . . ."

"No, you're *not* thinking—that's the problem!"

Suzanne began crying, and she pulled away from Don when he tried to comfort her.

"I'm sorry," he said. "I didn't mean it."

"I can't talk to you when you're like this," Suzanne sobbed while wiping the tears from her cheek with the back of her hand. "This isn't just about you. I have feelings, too, you know."

He took a deep breath and spoke slowly, with as much compassion as he could: "I know. But I *have* to put an end to this cruel joke of a family line, once and for all. Just like my parents should've done. I don't want to leave you alone, but *that* is not going to happen."

The next night, Don saw Robert in his dreams for the first time since their initial meeting.

"So you talked to a lawyer," said Robert.

Don wondered how it was possible for this man in his dreams to know what had happened in his waking hours. Then it came to him in a flash: "Oh, I get it. You're just a figment of my imagination. You're not really your own person, are you? I've just created you with my subconscious mind in order to help work through some issues. Classic psychology."

"Don't be silly—of course I'm my own person. It's true we're all connected in one continuous energy field, but I understand you well enough to know that's not what you meant."

"Then how did you know I went to see a lawyer? And why do you look just like me?"

"Don't think too much. You're going to need to trust me if this is going to work. You need to use your heart, not your head. I want you to get quiet right now and feel what's happening. Doesn't your intuition know that what I'm saying is true?"

Don closed his eyes and tried to tune in to his heart. It wasn't something he was used to, but once he was completely open to what he was feeling, there was a knowing . . . a complete understanding that what Robert was saying was indeed true. His mind continued to doubt, but the knowing emanating from his heart filled his entire being, and he felt unusually at peace with that knowledge.

When Don opened his eyes, he saw Robert standing in front of him. He still *looked* like Don himself, but there was a glow surrounding him that was much different.

"I have a question," said Don after a long pause.

"What would you like to know?"

"Why do I keep seeing clocks with the time of exactly 11:11? Does that mean anything?"

"Of course it does," replied Robert. "The universe has a long history of using different signs to grab the attention of people who are on their spiritual path. And in recent history, it's become quite common for the universe to use clocks as signposts to reassure people they're on the right track."

"Like a burning bush?"

"Let's hope you don't have to see a burning bush before you pay attention."

"Yeah," laughed Don. "What would the neighbors think?"

Robert smiled. "Until your intuition becomes stronger, the universe will give you periodic hints to let you know that you are *in the flow.*"

"'In the flow'? What does that mean?"

"In the flow of the universe. In some ways it's remarkably similar to a river. For example, if you lie down on the bank of a river, you won't go anywhere. But if you surrender to the current within the river itself, you can travel for miles without any effort. And the *flow* is the current of our destiny."

"Everybody always talks about the difference between destiny and free will. I guess you don't believe in free will."

"I absolutely believe in free will—unfortunately."

"Why is that unfortunate?"

"Because the universe has a well-crafted plan for everyone, and most of us ignore it our entire lives. We are so arrogant that we think we know more than anyone else about what's better for ourselves, and therefore we do everything we can to try to *force* our will into existence. Which is why most people struggle with life so much—they are so busy trying to live a life they think they want, instead of surrendering to the one that has already been destined for them."

"So, following your destiny is easier than exercising free will?"

"Absolutely."

"Well, I guess I'm lucky," said Don sarcastically. "I guess my life will be much easier now that I'm in the flow."

"It doesn't necessarily mean you're going to *like* your destiny; it just means it will be easier to get where you're destined to go. But more important, you can never take your destiny for granted. Destiny isn't a destination—it's a path. You can follow your destiny every day for a week, a month, or even a year and then fall out of it in a matter of seconds. What *is* lucky is that right now you've been given signs to reassure you that you're on the right path. But don't get too used to them, because soon they'll disappear."

"How will I know I'm on the right path after I stop seeing 11:11?"

"You'll need to develop your intuition, and then you'll be able to feel it without any external cues."

Although Don wasn't fully convinced that his life was predestined, it had begun to make more sense once Robert explained that he still had choice whether to follow what had been planned or not. Sometimes Don wished there was an instruction manual that explained how life really worked. It seemed unfair that he'd had to wait until he was about to die before learning how he should have lived.

"Okay," said Robert, "let's get on with it. Unfortunately, your physical pain will be getting a lot worse very shortly."

It didn't take much for Don to believe this. The burning in his esophagus had returned during the past week, and the pain had begun to spread throughout his abdomen.

"You have a choice," Robert continued. "You can live with the pain and let the cancer take its natural course—which will not be easy. Or you can find another doctor who will agree to treat you without insurance. Dr. Bernstein *had* to treat you at first because you were a referral from the emergency room. But since you haven't paid him, he's no longer obligated to continue. I'm sure there are doctors somewhere who will treat you for free, but there isn't one in Eugene. And you know what the lawyer told you about their fees."

"That Suzanne will have to pay for everything after I'm gone."

Robert nodded.

"But isn't there another option?" Don couldn't escape the feeling that there was something else he could do.

"Good—you're listening to your inner voice. However, I think you already know what the third option is. That's the real reason I'm here, isn't it?"

Don felt a chill run up his spine to the back of his neck. He *did* know what the third option was. He had been trying to avoid it at all costs because of Suzanne, but at this point he felt that he ultimately didn't have a choice. "I could end my own life," he whispered.

"Is that what you want?"

Now that Don had finally said it out loud, he knew there was only one answer. "Yes," he said after a long silence. "I think that's the best thing to do."

"Okay, then. We'd better get started while you still have your strength."

CHAPTER FIVE

Over the next three days, Don diligently followed Robert's detailed instructions. He was surprised by how meticulous the preparations were and concluded that this probably wasn't the first time Robert had done this.

The most unusual request Robert made was that Don get Suzanne a canine companion to be with her after he left. And it wasn't supposed to be just any dog, but a very specific one—a female black Lab named Sadie.

Suzanne had wanted to get a dog ever since they'd moved into their own house, but Don wasn't convinced. He hadn't wanted to be burdened with the responsibility of feeding and walking one every day in case they wanted to travel. Neither of them were particularly passionate about traveling, but Don always had the fantasy of going to the various local festivals around the world: the running of the bulls in Spain, Carnival in Brazil, the Day of the Dead in Mexico—that sort of thing.

However, when Don saw how Suzanne's eyes lit up when he suggested they get a dog, he wished they would have welcomed one into their family years ago.

They decided to go to the animal shelter first before visiting a pet store. The idea that they could save an unwanted animal from a tragic fate appealed to them both, and Don was almost as giddy as Suzanne on the way to the pound.

"Are you sure you know where it is?" Don asked.

"Of course I am. I drive past it on the way to work."

"I bet you stop by every day on your lunch break," he joked.

"If I did, there wouldn't be any room for you by now."

They both laughed, which felt really good. The excitement of bringing home a dog temporarily lifted the heaviness that had been hovering over them.

"Who's Robert?" Suzanne asked after a comfortable silence.

Don felt the blood rush from his face, and he turned completely pale. He hadn't ever spoken Robert's name out loud, and it was startling to hear Suzanne say it. He quickly reached over to the radio and turned up the volume. "I love this song."

"Who's Robert?" she repeated.

"I don't know a Robert." Don feigned contemplation. "Why do you ask?"

"Because you've been yelling his name every night for the past week in your sleep. Was he a childhood friend or something?"

"Hmm . . . no, I don't think so." Don felt like he had been caught in a lie and didn't know how to get out of it.

"Okay, I was just wondering. Maybe I didn't hear you right."

"I don't remember anyone named Robert from my past." He found it much easier to remain convincing while qualifying his answer so specifically. "Maybe it's an imaginary dog I used to play with as a kid." Don tried to force a laugh that didn't come out sounding natural.

"Yeah, maybe," Suzanne said incredulously.

Thankfully they were nearly to the pound, and Don was relieved that Suzanne dropped the subject as soon as they pulled into the driveway.

"Let's get a puppy!" she exclaimed. She slammed the door and ran toward the entrance of the white-planked building, with Don trailing behind.

"We're looking to adopt," Suzanne announced to the teenage volunteer who greeted them.

"Dogs to the left; cats to the right," the volunteer said in a squeaky voice as she waved toward the kennels in the back. "You can spend as much time as you like, but don't open the cages yourself. Most of the guests are very sweet, but a few are kinda cranky. Once you've decided, come and get me and I'll let you in."

When they entered the canine section, they saw rows of kennels on either side of them. The floor-to-ceiling chain-link fence and the narrow cement walkway made it feel unusually impersonal.

"This is depressing," Suzanne remarked.

Don nodded. As they walked in between the kennels, the reaction they got from the residents alternated between silent indifference and thunderous barking.

"They're all full grown," she said without hiding her disappointment. "I was hoping to get a puppy."

"Maybe there's one on the other side."

At the end of the long row of kennels was a blue cloth divider that separated the front of the kennel from the back. Don pulled it aside and gestured for Suzanne to go ahead. Many of the kennels on the other side were empty, and when they were nearly to the end, Don looked over at his wife and saw that her eyes were beginning to water. He instinctively put his arm around her while she cried.

"I just wanted a puppy." Her voice cracked through the tears. "Why can't I have a puppy?" She leaned against the cages and slid down until she was seated on the floor. Don sat next to her and gently caressed her hair.

"We can go to a pet store after this. I'm sure they'll have puppies there."

At that moment a whimper came from behind them, and something nudged Suzanne's back. When she turned around, she looked at a shiny black dog that was pushing its wet nose through the chain-link fence. And although the dog was fully grown, Don noticed that it retained some of its puppylike features.

"How are you?" asked Suzanne. "Are you uncomfortable in there?"

The dog whimpered again and began to lick Suzanne's face through the fence.

"Oh, she's the cutest thing. Do you want to come home with us today?" She opened the latch on the kennel and let the black dog into the hallway.

"She said we were supposed to ask before opening the kennels," Don said while looking around.

"It's okay, isn't it, girl?"

The dog walked around Suzanne and Don three times, deliberately looking at them from all angles before sitting down immediately in front of Suzanne. The dog offered its paw to her as a formal introduction and appeared to smile. Suzanne sat down so they were face-to-face and shook the paw, a huge smile overtaking her face.

It was the first time Don had seen that particular smile in months. It wasn't forced at all and didn't have an ounce of irony or trepidation behind it. He could also see that the crow's-feet around his wife's eyes had deepened, and the wrinkles at the corners of her mouth had become more pronounced from a life of hard living. It was as if moments like these meant much more because of all they were going through.

Don instantly tensed up as he saw the volunteer walking toward them. He was sure they'd done something wrong, but it looked like she was used to it.

"I see you met Sadie," the volunteer said in a chipper voice.

A chill went down the back of Don's neck. "What did you say her name was?"

"Sadie," the volunteer repeated.

"That's such a cute name," said Suzanne. "Do you want to come home with us, Sadie?"

"I'm afraid I have some bad news," said the volunteer. "Sadie's pregnant, so you probably don't want her. Is this your first dog?"

"Yes, it's our first dog, but what's wrong with being pregnant?" asked Suzanne indignantly. "Of course we want her."

Sadie put her head in Suzanne's lap and closed her eyes while her muzzle was gently stroked.

"You can adopt her if you want, but most first-time parents don't want to be grandparents so soon."

"When is she due?" asked Don.

"Very soon—I think in the next couple of weeks."

"We'll take her," said Suzanne. "Come on, Sadie. Let's go home."

Sadie and Suzanne went out to the car while Don filled out some paperwork with the volunteer at the reception desk. As he approached the car, there was something he hadn't seen before in Suzanne's eyes: a sense of purpose that seemed to unlock an energy deep within her soul.

Motherhood looked very good on her.

CHAPTER SIX

I n the days after they brought Sadie home, Robert was nowhere to be found in Don's dreams. The doppelgänger had previously given additional instructions whenever Don had completed a task, and his absence was unusual.

With every passing night, Don's health continued to deteriorate. He'd begun to cough up blood every morning, but fortunately it was easy to conceal the ugly effects of cancer from Suzanne when she was preoccupied with Sadie.

On the fifth day after they returned from the animal shelter, Robert finally visited Don when he was taking an afternoon nap.

"Where have you been?" asked Don.

"I've been making final preparations. Are you ready?"

"Definitely ready—the pain is unbearable now! I've been tempted to throw caution to the wind and begin treatments."

"Now is your last chance. There's nothing wrong with living. But you need to let me know, since today is the day."

"Today is the day?" Don felt a combination of sadness and excitement. He realized he hadn't said his proper goodbyes to Suzanne and wondered if he'd be able to.

"Yes, you'll be able to say goodbye." Robert seemed to read his mind. "But today is it. Your window will be open later tonight, and it's the only time I'll be able to help you through. Are you sure you want to go ahead with it?"

For a moment Don felt a sliver of apprehension, but the pain had begun to permeate his dream state, and he felt a stabbing sensation in his abdomen. "I'm sure," he finally replied. "What's next?"

"We need to decide how your physical body will be taken care of. I assume you want to inconvenience Suzanne as little as possible?"

Don had thought about that before, and he cringed when he imagined his wife coming across his body. He played through various scenarios in his head and could imagine the look of horror on her face when she discovered him. He was hoping there was a way to make it as quick and painless as possible, but the more he thought about it, the more he felt that his first priority was to make sure Suzanne wouldn't be traumatized.

"I don't want Suzanne to have to do anything," Don finally said. "Is that possible?"

"Yes, of course it's possible."

"How am I going to do it?" He thought of a gun. Pills. A razor blade. Exhaust fumes. Everything he could think of would leave Suzanne with his body to take care of. He didn't want her to have to deal with it at all. If there was a way for him to instantaneously disappear, that would be optimal.

"I know you've thought of several less-elegant solutions, but I think the best option for you would be a car crash."

Don thought about it for a moment and quickly agreed. His Land Cruiser was paid for, and although he loved it dearly, it wasn't worth much money. If he did it right, it would happen instantly and his physical remains would burn away without a trace. Either way, Suzanne wouldn't have to deal with his body in their home. It seemed perfect.

"Unfortunately, there's one big problem," Robert continued. "Even in your state it will be nearly impossible to pull off because of the innate 'fight-or-flight response' inherent in every human. A premeditated car crash takes several seconds of intense resolve. First, to get the car up to speed, and then to drive deliberately toward the fatal edge."

"I can do it," Don said confidently.

"I'm not so sure—it's really not that easy. I'm certain you'd be able to do yourself serious damage, but actually going all the way is pretty hard. One moment of doubt can make the difference between death and being in a coma for the rest of your life."

Don was horrified when he thought of being in a coma. Not only would he no longer be in control of his own life, but the medical bills would pile up on Suzanne, which would defeat the whole purpose. Don began to get angry. "Then why did you bring it up? What's the point if it's not possible?"

"It's very possible, but you're going to need some help."

"I thought that's what you were for."

"It's true I'm able to help you—but you needed to understand why."

"Okay." Don had begun to feel manipulated. "How can you help?"

"I'm going to need to take over."

"Take over what? You want to drive? Go ahead—there's just one little problem . . . you don't have a body!"

"Exactly. You have to let me take over your body so I can drive without worrying about living or dying."

Don wasn't sure he believed him, but there was something strangely confident about the way Robert was talking. He was now positive that he was being manipulated, but he didn't care. The whole point was that he was going to die anyway, so it didn't really matter. "Whatever. Fine. How do we do that?"

"All you have to do is agree, and we can start now. I'm in your mind when you're sleeping, but you need to give me permission to be present when you're awake. We'll both be inside your body at the same time, but I'll take over when we get behind the wheel."

"How do I know that I can trust you?"

"That's a very good question. You need to be confident that it's really what you want to do. This is a sacred agreement and can't be made with even a modicum of doubt."

Don didn't know if he could trust Robert and wondered if it was possible to tolerate the pain just a little while longer for the sake of being with Suzanne until the end. But although he wasn't sure if he could trust his doppelgänger, he was less sure if he could trust himself. His esophagus was now excruciatingly painful nearly every second of the day, and he had a vague recollection of a disturbing event that had happened when his pain had reached a new peak.

On a recent afternoon when the stabbing sensation in his throat had become so intense that he couldn't see more than a few inches from his face, there was something that snapped in him and he no longer felt in control of his actions. He remembered feeling an overwhelming desire to get rid of the pain by any means necessary, and he stumbled into the kitchen and began to search for the sharpest knife they had in order to cut the pain out of his throat. Although he didn't actually hurt himself seriously and the details were fuzzy, one thing was for certain: when he awoke on the floor, all of the knives in the butcher block were strewn around the kitchen and there were small cuts all over the palms of his hands.

Luckily Don had returned to consciousness before Suzanne had come home, because he was sure she would have rushed him to the hospital, which would have ruined everything that he had been working for.

Don didn't know *who* he could trust to ensure that he would never return to the hospital, but he knew without a doubt that he couldn't trust himself. He needed to end his life as soon as possible, before he did something that he couldn't undo.

"I trust you, Robert," he sighed after realizing that there was no one else he *could* trust. "Do whatever you need to do."

"Good. When you awake, we'll both be in your body. And then we can complete the final preparations."

When Don awoke from his nap, he had the uncomfortable feeling that someone was lying on top of him. The pain from his cancer had progressively gotten worse, but this was different. He felt as if he was submerged in water and was trying to breathe through a straw. He kept trying to push his way to the surface of his body, but it was nearly impossible.

Don began to panic while gasping for air, and he started to convulse. He tried to scream out loud, but no sound would come out of his mouth. Finally, after convulsing for nearly a minute, he broke through to the surface of his skin and sucked in several breaths of air. Slowly his heart rate returned to normal as he calmed down.

He heard a familiar voice coming from behind him.

"Are you okay?"

He turned around and didn't see anyone in the room.

"Who's there?" Don's panic returned as the sound of his voice echoed off the walls of his bedroom.

"It's Robert."

"Where are you?"

"I'm inside, just like you are. I know it's strange, but you'll get used to it pretty quickly."

Don began to remember what had happened when he was asleep and concluded that he must still be unconscious.

"Oh, I get it—I'm still dreaming."

"No, you're very much awake." Robert sounded annoyed. "You agreed this is what you wanted. Do you want me to help you or not?"

The reality of the situation returned to Don. "Yes, sorry. Of course I want your help. It's just that it doesn't feel real."

"This is probably the most real you've felt in years."

Don wasn't sure what Robert meant by that.

"And another thing," Robert continued. "There's no need to use your outside voice when talking to me. Remember I'm also inside, so I can hear your thoughts as soon as you think them. You don't want to worry Suzanne when she comes home and hears you talking to yourself."

"Why was it so hard to breathe at first?" Don asked silently.

"Sorry about that. I took the *first position* when I came in, and that will take you some time to get used to. It's perfectly safe, but I know it feels strange if you don't know what's happening. Surrender takes the most strength of any other practice. And surrendering inside your own body is the most difficult of all. Once I realized what was happening, I took the *second position,* which felt more natural for you."

"But I couldn't breathe."

"That's because you didn't need to—I was breathing for you. You'll get used to it pretty quickly, but I'll let you remain in first position for a little while longer while we wrap up the details."

Don wondered how long it would take before he would learn to surrender inside his own body.

When he'd first woken up, he felt like he was dying, but then he realized that was the whole point. It also dawned on him that Robert was probably right about his fight-or-flight response. There was something ingrained in his body that was determined to stay alive no matter what his brain wanted. Don finally came to the conclusion that he absolutely needed Robert's help and was now positive he wouldn't be able to pull it off alone.

"Are you still up for it?"

"I *think* so," Don said after a moment of silence.

"You better *know* so, because tonight's the night. Are you absolutely sure? You can still get out of it, but there's not much time left to change your mind."

"I'm sure. What's next?"

"Okay. Find a pen and paper and write down your final thoughts for Suzanne. Tell her why you're doing this, that you love her, and that everything will be okay."

Don went to the living room and opened the drawer of Suzanne's yellow desk to retrieve a small sheet of gold-leafed paper. Don had bought the stationery for her on her birthday a couple of years back. Although he knew that she loved the paper, it looked like she still hadn't used any of it. They both had a habit of saving "special" items indefinitely, instead of enjoying them in their daily lives. Don considered looking for a plain sheet of paper, but came to the conclusion that *this* particular letter was definitely stationery worthy.

When Don was confronted with the blank sheet of paper, he found that he didn't know what to say. Nothing he could think of seemed to carry the weight of the situation. He couldn't just say something flippant like "Thanks. See you later." Writing a suicide note was much harder than he'd thought it would be.

"Just write from your heart," said Robert. "Don't worry about the words; just write down your feelings."

Don was still getting used to hearing Robert's voice inside his head when he was awake, and it startled him once again. He was starting to grow comfortable with the claustrophobic feeling of two souls inhabiting one body, but the voice always took him by surprise. It came from deep within his body, and although he knew nobody else could hear it, it sounded like it echoed throughout the entire house.

Don began by revisiting some of his favorite memories of Suzanne since they had been together.

When they first met. The first time they made love. Their vacation to the Oregon coast. A candlelit dinner on the floor of their furniture-free new house. And several images of Suzanne's beautiful hazel eyes and the way they sparkled when she smiled.

When the revisitation of memories was over, Don looked down at the stationery and saw that the letter had essentially been written. The words floated above the page, hovering in space and waiting to be committed to paper. He picked up the pen and began to trace them slowly—one letter at a time. After he was finished, he carefully folded the sheet of paper in half and sealed it inside a matching envelope. On the front he wrote in his most legible script: "Dearest Suzanne."

"Good," said Robert. "Put the letter in a safe place. You'll need it tonight."

Don noticed that the sky had become dark as he hid the letter in the back of the desk drawer. After replacing the drawer, he heard the familiar sound of Suzanne's key sliding into the front-door lock.

"Hi, hon," she said when she entered the room. "How are you feeling?"

"Pretty tired." Writing the letter had taken more out of him than he thought it would.

"Sorry I'm late. We had to do month-end reconciliations before the partner meeting tomorrow. Are you up for eating tonight?"

The thought of food turned Don's stomach. He hadn't eaten very regularly during the past week, and with Robert inside him, he didn't feel there was any *room* for anything else.

"No, that's okay. You go ahead."

"They bought us all Chinese, so I'm good. But I can make you something. How about some toast?"

"Really, I'm fine. I'm not hungry."

"You need to eat something"—she yawned—"even if it's a cracker. I guess I should get to bed—I have to go in early tomorrow to make copies before the meeting."

Don made his way across the room and hugged his wife as tightly as he could. The pressure of the embrace made the pain in his chest shoot through his body with an intensity that he hadn't felt before. And although it was nearly unbearable, he held on to her as long as he could. He tried to say in silence what he could never put into words: that their love was eternal; that she was and would always be his entire world; but most important, that he was sorry . . . deeply sorry for what he was about to do.

When he could no longer tolerate the pain of their final embrace, he slowly pulled away and attempted to wipe the tears from his face before his wife saw them.

"Are you okay?" Suzanne asked tenderly.

"I'm just tired."

Suzanne smiled sweetly and gently squeezed his hand. "Are you coming to bed?" she asked, and began to make her way down the hallway.

"I'll be right there."

Don sighed deeply and took a moment to look around the home they had made together. The kitchen table, the living-room couch, the coffee table. The *life* they had made together. He wondered if he was doing the right thing by leaving his wife in this way. Was it selfish? He had always heard that suicide was selfish and that everyone who survived would be hurt. But Suzanne was the only family he had left to speak of. He had a few acquaintances, but nobody he would consider a real friend. Suzanne was all that mattered, and he was doing it for her. She would be sad at first, but eventually she would be thankful when she realized why he had done it.

Don deliberately walked across the kitchen one last time and slid open the silverware drawer slowly, closing his eyes and hoping he had imagined the contents. But when he opened his eyes again, they were still there: stacks of medical bills that he was leaving for his wife to pay. But thankfully there would be no more. He was putting an end to the accrual of more debt, and one day she would be thankful.

He was doing it for her.

CHAPTER SEVEN

"Wake up," said Robert. "It's time to get up!"

Startled, Don sat up and looked around for the voice before he realized what was happening.

"You fell asleep," Robert continued. "The time is now—let's go!"

Don looked at his sleeping wife, and his throat began to constrict until he felt like he was no longer able to breathe. As he gasped for air, the pain in his heart became more intense than all of his cancer put together. He couldn't believe *he* was the one who was going to leave her. Suzanne was the only person who had ever really loved him, and he couldn't imagine living without her. If he wasn't going to take his own life, being alone without her would surely have killed him.

"We don't have any more time," Robert whispered.

Don closed his eyes tightly and ran through all of the scenarios in his head one last time. When he once again reached the same conclusion he had every other time, another stabbing pain shot through his chest and he doubled over on the bed. After the throbbing wave finally passed, he opened his eyes and saw Suzanne sleeping peacefully. Tears streamed down his face, and he covered his mouth to muffle the cries so he wouldn't wake her. "I'm sorry," he cried softly. "I love you so much."

The air in the house felt like quicksand as he slipped out of bed and slowly made his way across the room. Shutting the door behind him as quietly as he could, he stood in the hallway for a few seconds when he realized that he had just left their bedroom for the last time.

Don found his keys on the kitchen counter, and he made his way to the garage through the inside door off the living room. Although his car was parked on the street, he wanted to use the side door of the garage so he wouldn't wake Suzanne.

After turning on the garage light, he looked at the unpacked boxes from their previous apartment.

I should have cleaned up the garage before I left, he thought. *I guess it's too late now.*

As he walked toward the outside door, he thought he heard a squeaking sound coming from under the workbench. The sound stopped as soon as he walked toward it, but when he turned around, he heard the squeaking again.

"Damn rats!" he said as he spun around and looked under the workbench for the rodent.

Out of the corner of his eye, Don noticed a cardboard box that was rocking back and forth. As he edged closer, he could see that the contents were strewn across the floor, and the newspaper packing material had been shredded. Cautiously, he grabbed a broom that was leaning up against the wall and held it on the bristle side while using the handle to lift open the flap of the fallen box. He saw a familiar black tail protruding from the opening.

"Sadie, is that you?"

Don sat down in front of the box just in time to see a tiny black puppy being born. Sadie instinctively licked the shiny birth sac off the newborn and gently nudged the puppy to join its siblings, which were already beginning to nurse. Don counted five wrinkled black puppies that were happily squeaking and squirming amongst one another. He was struck by how innately nurturing Sadie was, and wondered how she knew precisely what to do. The volunteer at the pound had mentioned that she was a first-time mother—it was incredible to watch firsthand how nature takes care of itself.

After a few minutes of watching the newborns enjoy their first meal, Don began to get up. "Welcome to the world," he said as he stood upright. "I guess it's my time to leave."

"Sit down," said the familiar voice inside his head. "I want to talk to you about something very important."

Startled, Don sat back down and said, "You have to stop doing that—you scared the death out of me."

"We'll see about that," Robert quipped.

"Bad choice of words."

"Maybe not. That's what I want to talk to you about."

Don didn't understand and began to feel anxious. "Shouldn't we get going? Suzanne will hear us out here and come to see what's going on."

"She's still sound asleep. Just listen for a few minutes, and we'll be on our way shortly."

"Okay, talk."

"First of all let me say I will absolutely honor my word and help you transition in the manner we previously discussed."

"Uh-huh." Don squinted incredulously. "But?"

"But, first I want to talk to you about the implications of what you're doing."

"I already know the implications. I'm going to die in order to stop my suffering *and* stop the senseless acquisition of debt. Suzanne will be sad at first, but over time she'll understand that it wasn't selfish at all, since she won't have to pay any more money to the stupid doctors who can't even save me."

"Yes, those are the physical implications. But life is more complex than just what happens on Earth. There are serious soul implications of suicide."

"Oh, great, now you're going to get religious on me. What, am I going to hell now?" Don was starting to get angry. "Don't you think this *is* a living hell? I have flippin' cancer, and I can't even pay for the treatment without ruining the love of my life's financial future! All because of some stupid political statement that nobody even cared about!" The veins in Don's neck began to protrude, and his face turned bright red.

Robert let him finish and then calmly replied, "I don't know anything about hell—that's really not my thing. But I *do* know that souls have their own time frame, and *they* are the ones who are traditionally responsible for deciding when it's time to die."

"Well, this time I'm deciding. Are you going to help me or not?"

"As I said before, I will help you in any way you want. Just listen to me for a few more minutes, and then we can go."

"Okay, I'm sorry. Go on."

"You might think that your body is in control, but ultimately it's not. Your soul has its own path independent of which body it inhabits. The soul makes an agreement with a particular body before it's born to help accomplish its goals."

"If that's true, why would my soul pick a body that was going to get cancer? Is my soul *stupid*, or does it just have a sick sense of humor?"

"Good question. There are many reasons why souls pick different bodies. The short answer is: because there is something very important to learn from them. Profound growth comes from overcoming adversity, and a soul that chooses a body with severe physical limitations is usually preparing to learn some very significant lessons during that particular lifetime."

"Okay, I've learned my lesson: cancer sucks. Next."

"Unfortunately, it's not your decision what lesson you are to learn during this lifetime. Besides, I'm a hundred percent confident you *haven't* learned it yet."

"Why do you say that?"

"Because you're not dead. If you were through learning, your soul would have already pulled the plug and you'd be on your way."

Don's frustration was deepening as he put his elbows on his knees and his head in his hands.

"Obviously you have free will," Robert continued, "and ultimately you can end your body's life. But since you'll be short-circuiting your current journey on Earth, your soul won't have accomplished what it came here to do. And it's a shame, too, especially after all that you've gone through. I would argue that you've gone through the worst of it already. Didn't your doctors say you only had a few months left?"

"Three to six months."

"Right. So you've endured thirty-nine years, and you're going to risk having to learn all these lessons over again so you can save a few months. It doesn't make any sense to me."

"But isn't there a time when suicide is a noble act?" asked Don. "Absolutely the right thing to do for everyone involved?"

"Yes, it's possible. It really depends on the individual situation. If taking one's life is completely selfless—entirely motivated by love—then it's feasible that the soul's journey on Earth will be fulfilled."

"So that's what I'll say. I'm doing this for Suzanne—I won't run up any more pointless doctors' bills."

"It's not a negotiation, Don. You can't talk your way out of this. I believe that you're genuinely concerned about money, but it doesn't feel to me like it's coming from a selfless place. Are all of your money concerns simply about protecting Suzanne? Or is there something else that's under all those feelings?"

"How would I know that?" Don asked indignantly.

"You know in your heart. If there is even a sliver of doubt, then you know what I'm saying is true."

"But the pain is unbearable."

"I understand it's excruciating to be in your body right now, but maybe there is another option to consider."

"What's that?"

"We can get you a new body, and I'll take over this one."

"Very funny."

"I'm serious. If you stay on Earth, you won't erase the lessons you've already learned. And then you can continue to walk your current path without being burdened by the pain and suffering of cancer."

"But the cancer will still be there. How are *you* going to deal with that?"

"First of all, I have a much higher threshold for pain than you do. But more important, since I won't be attached to the underlying emotional trauma that created the cancer in the first place, I'll probably be able to transcend it altogether."

"You think you can heal my cancer?"

"Probably."

"Then why don't you just do it now so I can live a long, healthy life in my own body? You're already inside anyway. If you can cure cancer, then just do it now."

"It's not that easy. Whether you want to or not, you're still holding on to the root causes of it. In fact, the cancer is embedded in your soul. Your soul had a contract before you were born to use cancer as a tool of learning in this lifetime. There's nothing I can do to separate you from your cancer."

"Does that mean I'll get cancer again in a new body? If so, what's the point?"

"Another great question. I really don't know the answer to that. However, it doesn't seem very likely. It actually takes quite a lot of energy to summon a fatal illness such as cancer, and since the disease itself isn't the real reason you got sick, it probably won't happen again. That's why this idea might be your best option. You'll still have access to the energetic lessons that result from being conscious on the same plane as your disease, but you won't have to deal with the suffering."

"And what do *you* get out of it?"

"I get a body that I can use to accomplish what I need to do on Earth."

"Why don't you just get a *new* body that doesn't have cancer? Be born just like the rest of us."

"To save time. You can already walk and talk. A new body takes several years to mature enough to do what I need to do. And it's also convenient that you're already living in the United States, which is where I need to be right now."

"To do what?"

"Many things. Healing mostly. This is an important time for the spiritual development of the entire human race. And because of its relatively short history, the U.S. hasn't been able to develop spiritually as fully as other parts of the world. That's why there are so many of us coming here right now—to impart our wisdom and allow this country to catch up with the rest of the world."

"Us? Who's 'us'? There are others taking over cancer victims' bodies? Are you some alien race or something?"

"No," Robert laughed. "We're called *Walk-ins*. It's not that unusual, really. We're simply angels that need to have a body to accomplish what we have to do. It's been going on for thousands of years, but it's most commonly prearranged before the host body is born. So this conversation doesn't usually take place here on Earth. But I have a soft spot for suicide victims. Someone very close to me killed herself, and not only did it hurt me deeply, but I saw firsthand what happened to her soul. She's still trying to recover from it, and it's already been many lifetimes since it happened."

"I'm sorry."

"Thank you, but it's the way it's meant to be. It's her destiny, and she's living it with as much grace and determination as she can. It's such a shame, though. Such a waste of time. Having to pay for a moment of release with lifetimes of additional suffering. So that's why I do what I do. Trust me, it's much easier to simply make a contract with a relatively healthy soul before it's born. But I prefer to spend the extra effort to work with souls like yours, to hopefully prevent lifetimes of suffering that can be avoided."

"Wow," said Don. "That's pretty incredible."

"So you have a decision to make: we can continue with the original plan, or we can find you a new body and I can take over this one."

"Okay, I'm in," Don replied after thinking for several seconds. "Let's do the swap. But where are we going to find a body that I can use?"

"We already have." Robert used his will to gesture toward Sadie.

"A dog! You want me to become a dog? Are you crazy? Aren't there any human bodies I can use?"

"I'm afraid that's your only option. I've been working hard to arrange it for you, and there simply isn't any more time to find another body. As you can imagine, human bodies are in quite high demand at the moment. And besides, you need to be near me for as long as possible in order to fulfill your soul's contract. Therefore, being a dog is the most practical option since I don't have the time to carry around a newborn human. They take much longer to develop."

Don grumbled out loud.

"It's actually not so bad," Robert continued. "I've been a dog several times myself. You get to accomplish a lot in a relatively short amount of time."

"I don't know . . ."

"Well, you have to decide quickly. There's only one more opportunity left. There are eight pups in the litter, and the last one is on its way now."

Don counted seven puppies nuzzling against Sadie. "They *are* awfully cute."

"That's as good a reason as any." Robert laughed. "You wouldn't be the first to choose a body based on its appearance."

Don felt slightly offended by Robert's offhand comment, but the more he thought about it, the more he liked it. "I guess it's better to be a dog since they don't live as long. Then I can move on more quickly."

"That's true. So are you ready?"

"Yes, but you need to promise me one thing."

"What's that?" asked Robert.

"That you won't touch Suzanne. I want her to be happy and eventually find someone else, but it creeps me out to think you'd be with her in my old body."

"I completely understand. You have my word. Anything else?"

"No, that's it."

"Okay, let's begin. Lie down on your back next to Sadie—then close your eyes and breathe deeply."

"Okay."

"Shhh. Don't say anything. Relax your mind and open your heart. Now, I want you to focus your energy on the top of your head—where your soft spot was as an infant. Concentrate on that point until it starts to feel warm."

Don concentrated on the top of his head until it became warm.

"Good. Now imagine the bones that came together to form your skull have started to become pliable again."

The thought of this made Don feel queasy at first, but he relaxed and imagined the top of his head beginning to soften. It was remarkably relaxing, and within a few minutes he felt like he was floating.

"Okay, stay open like that. Now I'm going to help you out of your body. Just relax. Remember this is perfectly natural—it's perfectly safe. I'll be with you the whole time."

Don began to feel nauseated, as if he had just eaten something that didn't agree with him. The feeling grew until he felt as if he had a huge ball in the pit of his stomach. The bloating was so pronounced that he almost opened his eyes to see if his belly was distended. But as quickly as it came, it dissipated and he felt an intense rush of energy flow from the base of his spine, travel down his legs, and accumulate in his feet. The energy warmed his feet, and his ankles began to throb in time with his pulse. His feet then started to swell, and when they felt like they had swollen up to three or four times their normal size, the energy shot back up his legs; up his spine; through his stomach, heart, and throat; and out the top of his head. As the energy traveled up his body, it felt like it was sweeping out every last bit of physical sensation he had left. By the time it reached his head, there was no feeling remaining in his body from the neck down.

Don hadn't realized how much he'd become used to the constant pain in his body until it was gone. It was as if a huge weight had been lifted from his torso, and he felt light and free for the first time in years. When he finally opened his eyes, he was surprised to find himself floating near the rafters of the garage. Looking down, he saw his body lying still below.

Don began to swirl in circles, faster and faster, until everything was a blur from spinning. Then, as if a huge vacuum was pulling him down, he was thrust toward the ground below, and immediately before reaching Sadie, he blacked out.

CHAPTER EIGHT

When morning came, Suzanne once again woke up to an empty bed. Ever since the diagnosis, Don's insomnia had gotten much worse, and she was becoming used to regularly waking up without him. She also hadn't slept very well because she had been disturbed by bad dreams all night. She couldn't remember exactly what they were, but it had something to do with her relationship with Don. Her dreams had been more and more upsetting in the past week, and she surmised that they stemmed from her anxiety surrounding Don's illness.

Once she was fully awake, Suzanne made her way to the kitchen, where she heard whimpering sounds coming from the garage. Knowing exactly what was making the noise, she excitedly flung open the door to the garage. On the floor was the most precious thing she could have imagined. Her husband was lying asleep with a tiny wrinkled puppy curled in a ball on his chest. Sadie was nearby inside a cardboard box, with seven puppies nursing enthusiastically. They sang a chorus of new-puppy sounds, alternating between grunting, slurping, and whimpering.

Suzanne stood in the doorway for several minutes while her face began to get sore from grinning so widely. She bent down and carefully scooped up the newborn puppy that had been sleeping on her husband's chest. She was able to nuzzle the soft fur with her nose and cheek before he started to wake up. The puppy squirmed and wiggled until she gently placed him next to his siblings. Instinctively, he began to nurse, clearly famished from his recent journey.

Suzanne smiled at her husband as he slowly opened his eyes and rubbed them with the back of his hand. He seemed to have a difficult time sitting up but finally managed by contorting himself sideways.

"Good morning, sunshine," Suzanne said to him sweetly.

"G-g-g," Robert attempted to respond to Don's wife. "M-m-m-orn-n."

Suzanne could see that her husband's yellowed eyes were sunken more deeply than they had been before. Clearly the cancer was progressing quickly, and it now seemed to be affecting his speech. She had been warned that Don's personality might start to degenerate if the cancer metastasized to his brain, and for the first time since he got sick, she began to wonder if she had the strength to see him through it. Her friends had advised her to put him in a hospital or at least hire an in-home hospice worker to take care of him, but she had promised Don that she wouldn't. However, seeing him having difficulty speaking that morning made her question her resolve.

"Did you see the birth?" she asked after a long pause.

"Y-y-e-s-s."

"Was it beautiful?"

Robert forced a cockeyed smile and nodded slowly.

Suzanne turned her attention to Sadie and crouched down near the new mother. "How are *you* doing, Mama? Did you have a long night?"

Sadie looked at Suzanne without moving her head. The dog had the distinct look of exhaustion and bliss that is shared among mothers. Suzanne felt a wave of sadness overcome her when she finally accepted that *she* wouldn't be able to experience motherhood, at least not with Don. She looked back at her husband, who had pulled himself up by grabbing on to the grille of her car. She considered helping him up, but he was much too proud. He would need to get over that soon enough, but she decided to leave him to his own devices a little while longer.

Robert used the wall to steady himself while shuffling into the house. When he reached the door, he turned his head and said as clearly as he could, "Y-y-ou s-s-tay here. I'm g-g-oing to b-b-ed."

As soon as her husband left, Suzanne burst into tears. She didn't know if she was strong enough to see him die a slow death. She wished he would agree to at least try the chemotherapy. Although the doctors said it wouldn't necessarily extend his life, it would likely make him more comfortable.

For the first time, Suzanne allowed herself to wonder how much time her husband had left. Judging by the way he was acting today, it didn't seem like very much longer.

"Soon it will just be us," she said to Sadie and the puppies while forcing a smile. "Just the ten of us."

"Wake up," whispered Suzanne. "Are you okay? Wake up, hon."

Robert opened his eyes and saw Don's wife come into focus. He could see the sense of relief in her eyes when he regained consciousness. And the love emanating from her heart was as pure as any he'd felt before. He was starting to understand why Don was prepared to do what he was going to do. If there was a love powerful enough to drive one to take one's own life, this was it.

"You've been sleeping for two days," Suzanne said while helping him sit up. "I was worried about you."

Robert attempted to speak, but his throat felt constricted. "W-w-a," he croaked.

"You must be dehydrated," Don's wife said while grabbing a glass of water from the nightstand. "Have some water."

Robert drained the entire glass in one long drink and gave it back to Suzanne. "Thank you," he said with a sigh. "I was thirsty."

"I see that," she smiled sweetly. "Are you okay? I was worried about you sleeping so much."

"I was just tired."

"Do you want something to eat?"

"Not hungry." Usually Robert was starving when he entered a new body, but for some reason the thought of food repulsed him.

Suzanne filled the glass with water again, and after returning it to the nightstand, she leaned over to kiss her husband. Robert recoiled and shook his head violently.

"What's wrong?"

Robert kept shaking his head until he thought of something to say. He had made a promise to Don that he intended to honor. Although he was sure there was no way Don would find out if Suzanne kissed him that morning, he wanted to be able to assure him that nothing had happened.

"Bad breath," he finally said with a wry smile. He remembered that humor often kept uncomfortable situations at bay.

"Okay," she laughed. "You're a nut."

"I'll be fine," he said, smiling. "Go to work, and I'll call you if I need anything."

Suzanne nodded while looking at her watch. "I better go now—I'm late." She blew him a kiss from across the room and ran out the door.

After Suzanne left, Robert began to feel the pain that Don had been harboring. It started as a dull throbbing throughout his torso and culminated in sharp stabbing pains in the area of his solar plexus. And his scratchy throat gave way to a burning sensation at the base of his esophagus whenever he swallowed.

"I need to work on the body first," he said aloud to nobody in particular. He could sense that the cancer was spreading rapidly, and it was important to get it under control soon or else the body would be of no use to him.

Robert knew from his previous Walk-in experiences that thoughts and memories were stored within the cells in the human body. This cellular memory was one of the reasons why being a Walk-in was so effective after the original soul was no longer inhabiting the body, and was how it already knew how to walk and talk. However, the body also stored *emotions* in its cells, especially if they hadn't been given the opportunity to be outwardly expressed in a healthy manner. Suppressed emotions often became trapped in the cells, which could ultimately result in disease. Robert assumed that this had likely contributed to Don's health problems, and he was hoping to find the core emotions that might have been trapped.

Closing his eyes, Robert started with the pain in the esophagus. He attempted to *feel into* Don's unexpressed emotions that were intertwined with the pain. At first he didn't feel anything other than a burning sensation, but as he progressed lower to the base of the stomach, he discovered a large pool of unexpressed *worry*. Initially, it seemed to be about the illness itself getting worse, but then he discovered a much bigger pool of unexpressed worry about *money*. Within the stomach, the worry about money was nearly paralyzing, and Robert was confident that it had contributed to the spread of the cancer there.

"I'm worried I don't have insurance!" Robert yelled at the top of his lungs. "I'm worried the medical bills are going to destroy us financially! I'm worried we'll lose our house because of my stupid disease!"

Robert felt deeply into the emotions that were trapped in his stomach, and they were all of a similar theme. Every time he felt a new one, he would express it out loud with as much strength as he could muster. "I'm worried I'll never be able to work again!" This realization was shocking even to Robert, and it sent chills down his spine. It was clear to him that Don had invested much of his personal self-worth in his career, and the thought that he would never be able to pursue it again absolutely horrified him.

"I'll never work again!" he yelled as loud as he could. "I'll never work again!" he kept screaming over and over until he began to cry. It started with a few tears welling up at the corners of his eyes, and within seconds it evolved into a full wail. He cried so hard that he began convulsing on the bed, and his sobs degenerated into dry heaves. He gasped for several minutes, clutching his stomach and writhing on the bed until his breath returned.

After the convulsions were finally over, Robert opened his eyes and focused on the ceiling fan until the rest of the room came back into focus. He could feel that the burning in his esophagus was significantly less, and the upper part of his abdomen felt much lighter.

He continued to release the trapped emotions that had lodged themselves deep within the cells of the various organs. In addition to the anxiety and worry in the pancreas and stomach, Don had squirreled away unexpressed fear in his kidneys, grief in his lungs, and anger in his liver. It was a miracle he had only been diagnosed with cancer of the pancreas, because several of his other organs were on the verge of succumbing to the fatal disease.

He wondered how society had evolved to the point of letting such self-destructive behavior become so common. In the name of harmony, humans had apparently begun to favor the suppression of one's own emotions over expressing them openly while they were still manageable. And, in addition to the self-inflicted tragedies similar to Don's, many more outwardly destructive tragedies were becoming commonplace as victims regularly lashed out at others when they were no longer able to contain their emotions. Sometimes the damage was limited to their own homes, but more frequently these tragedies were claiming larger and larger numbers of victims.

After several hours, Robert's hunger returned with a vengeance. He was famished, and went into the kitchen to find something to eat. Rummaging through the refrigerator, he found an unopened bag of baby carrots, and noticed that there was a half-eaten loaf of bread on the counter. He intuitively grabbed both and returned to the bedroom, where he proceeded to eat the entire bag of carrots and most of the bread in one sitting.

He felt the nourishing energy flow through his body, and although his stomach began to cramp once he had finished, thankfully he was able to keep the food down and enjoy the benefits. He didn't know exactly how long Don had gone without eating, but judging by how his body was reacting, it was probably quite some time.

Robert was still exhausted from the *worry* that he had released earlier in the morning, but he knew that he still had to get to the root of the cancer itself. He decided to take a quick nap to regain some of his energy before continuing, and slept without a single dream, which was unusual for him. When he was in the physical world, he often dreamed in order to stay in touch with his life on the spiritual plane. But this time, even his subconscious self was preoccupied with breaking down the nourishment that he had consumed before he fell asleep. He slept for most of the afternoon and was awakened by Suzanne when she came home from work.

"How are you feeling?" she asked as she was changing out of her work clothes.

Robert quickly averted his eyes and tried to casually focus on the glass of water he was drinking.

"What's wrong?" she asked. "Why won't you look at me?"

Robert wasn't uncomfortable with Suzanne changing, but he took Don's request seriously. Even under the best of circumstances, the sense of helplessness one felt after surrendering one's body to someone else could easily throw a soul into depression. Because of this, Robert knew it was important to go out of his way to distance himself from her as soon as possible.

Thinking quickly, Robert feigned a coughing fit and acted like he hadn't heard what Suzanne had asked. He continued to cough until his face turned beet red and the veins in his neck protruded. Suzanne rushed to his side and pounded his back repeatedly until he stopped coughing.

"Thanks," he said. "I think some water went down the wrong pipe."

"Are you better now?"

Robert nodded. "Good news—I ate some carrots and bread today."

"I see that," she said, looking at the empty wrappers on the nightstand. "There are crumbs everywhere." She smiled while brushing the crumbs off the bed with the edge of her hand. "Can I make you some dinner?"

"I'd love some more carrots," he said.

"I think you ate them all. Do you want me to go to the store?"

"If you don't mind."

"Do you want anything else?"

Robert tried to put a word to the specific hunger

he was feeling. "Fruit," he finally said. "And some more bread, please."

"Are you sure? You hate fruit. What kind do you want?"

Robert saw a vision of a particular fruit in his mind but couldn't retrieve the name of it. "I dunno, just fruit."

"'Just fruit,'" she mimicked. "Okay, I'll get you some carrots, bread, and some *just fruit*," she smiled. "I'll be right back."

Robert was waiting in the kitchen when Suzanne returned, and he systematically studied every morsel she removed from the shopping bag. When she was finished putting everything on the counter, he instinctively grabbed a medium-sized fruit with a smooth greenish red skin.

"Mango," said Suzanne. "You wanted a mango. Interesting. I thought you hated all fruit."

Robert brought the mango to his mouth and took a big bite as if it was an apple. The flavor was rich and sweet, but the peel was bitter and chewy.

"You're not supposed to eat the skin!" Suzanne exclaimed as she grabbed the fruit out of his hands. "Let me peel it for you." She giggled as she cut the skin off with a sharp paring knife.

The energy from the mango immediately entered Robert's bloodstream, and everything came into focus. Unfortunately, this heightened the awareness of the pain in his upper abdomen. He pressed as hard as he could between his ribs to apply pressure to the pancreas, but it didn't help. The pain quickly became unbearable, and he stumbled to the bedroom and got back into bed with Suzanne's help.

"Maybe you shouldn't have eaten the entire mango so quickly," she said.

Robert understood the real problem was that the pain in his stomach had masked the pain in the pancreas, and as he'd become stronger, he was able to feel the next threshold of pain. He knew that the next thing he had to do was to release the emotions that had been trapped in the pancreas, but it wasn't going to be easy. It would also be uncomfortable for Suzanne to watch, so he decided to wait until she was at work the following day.

Robert closed his eyes and pretended to be asleep while Suzanne changed into her nightclothes and quietly climbed into bed. After a few hours, he was able to fall asleep once his fatigue finally overtook the pain.

The next morning, Robert awoke to find that his nausea had dissipated, yet his hunger remained. He made his way to the kitchen and saw a note on the refrigerator door that was affixed with a ladybug magnet:

"Gotta do monthlies today. Cut fruit in the fridge.
— Love, S."

Robert opened the door and enjoyed the fruit plate that Suzanne had prepared for him. After eating, he visited the garage for the first time since the "swap." The puppies were all nuzzled against their mother, who was still clearly exhausted from all the excitement of the past few days.

Robert kneeled down next to Sadie and put his hand gently on the side of her muzzle. "Thank you, Sadie," he said telepathically. "You have done a very selfless and noble thing. Don and I are both forever in your debt."

Sadie took a deep breath and sighed.

"I need to take Don away for a little while, but I promise I'll take good care of him."

Sadie whimpered quietly and licked the small puppy that was sleeping third from her left.

Robert gently picked up the puppy she had kissed and cradled him with his right arm. "I'll bring him back soon," he said out loud. "Come on, Don. It's time to do some work."

Robert carried the small puppy to the bedroom and put him on the pillow at the head of the bed. He took a moment to smooth the teal-and-cream-colored comforter before lying down and placing the puppy on his chest. He watched the furry black baby rise and fall with his every breath before continuing.

"Okay, my friend. It's time to get to the root of all this," he said aloud to the puppy. "What are you *really* worried about, Don?"

"I think I'm blind!" exclaimed Don. Ever since he had been born into the puppy's body, he couldn't see anything.

"You're not blind." Robert laughed. "Your eyes just haven't opened yet."

Don felt relieved when he was reminded that puppies were born with their eyes closed. "Oh yeah, I forgot. That's normal, right?"

"Of course it's normal." Robert laughed again.

Don was still getting used to being in a puppy body. In some ways it was remarkably similar to being in a human one, with a few obvious differences. First of all, he could only walk around on four legs instead of two; related to this was the fact that he could no longer pick things up with his hands. This frustrated Don the most, although he discovered that there would always be another way of doing something that he was used to doing with his hands. For example, whenever his nose would itch, he found that his tongue was able to lick it, which felt remarkably more satisfying than scratching it with his fingers ever had. He spent hours at a time licking his nose with his warm tongue because of how good it felt.

But the thing that Don enjoyed the most was his tail. It seemed to be connected directly to his emotions and would express his feelings without him having to think about them. When he was feeling good, his tail would wag in a rhythm that forced his hips to move back and forth in what could only be described as a "happy dance." And when he was feeling upset, his tail would slap against whatever was near in a dramatic display of anger and discontentment. Suzanne had often complained that Don wouldn't show his feelings, and he couldn't help but think that she would be proud of him now. The more he thought about it, the more he realized that he had always expressed himself with his tail. However, when he was in a human body, his tail was simply too small to see.

"Okay, Don," said Robert. "I'm going to re-connect our energetic fields together so that we can feel each other's emotions. This isn't something I recommend doing on a regular basis, but we need to work together to release the toxic emotions that are embedded in your human body."

"I don't know what that means."

"It's simple, really. All it means is that you'll be able to feel your old human body once again as if you were still inside of it."

Within seconds Don began sensing the familiar pain of being inside of his human body. He was still aware of his puppy body, but there was an expanded awareness that included his old vessel. Once his awareness completely came into focus, Don couldn't help grimacing from the pain of his illness.

"Welcome back," said Robert. "What I'm going to do is guide you to different places within your old body where you have buried various emotions."

"What do *I* do?"

"You simply let me guide you, and when you come across an emotion, just feel it as deeply as you can. Don't run away from your feelings like you have for years—just feel them completely."

"Okay."

"And since I can feel what you're feeling," continued Robert, "I'm going to give voice to whatever emotions you come across, hopefully releasing them so they'll no longer continue to damage this body."

After a few seconds, Don felt an inner movement that was similar to being pushed through the snow on a sled. There was a thrilling sense of freedom as he moved faster and faster, and he was just starting to enjoy it when he felt a sharp pain in his pancreas. Almost immediately, the physical pain was replaced with fear and the familiar anxiety about money.

"How are we going to pay for these medical bills?" Robert yelled out loud, which startled Don. "Suzanne is going to hate me!" Robert screamed even louder. "She's going to hate me for ruining her life!"

Don began to worry whether someone could hear Robert yelling. Suzanne and Don were always pretty even-keeled, and when they occasionally disagreed, they would still communicate in relatively hushed tones.

"Nobody can hear us," Robert assured him. "Don't get distracted with being self-conscious. Just *feel into* the pain, and let whatever emotions come up flow freely."

"I'll try."

Don once again felt pushed into the center of the pain within his pancreas. This time he sensed his breathing stop as he heard one of his biggest fears uttered out loud for the first time in his life.

"She's going to hate me," screamed Robert, "and then she's going to leave me!"

This sent chills throughout Don's entire being.

"I'm worried that Suzanne will leave me, and then I'll die alone!"

Don was whisked from one painful place to another, deep within the organs of his previous body. He began to anticipate Robert's expression of his deepest fears, although it didn't make it any less startling when Don heard the actual words—especially when it came to Suzanne.

"She'll meet someone better looking, with more money. . . .

"She'll discover I'm a fraud . . . how damaged I am . . . that I'm lying . . . that I'm too clingy. . . .

"She'll see who I really am . . . and then she'll leave me!"

Don's head began to swirl, and he felt like he was going to be sick. Because his eyes were closed, he didn't have any sense of up or down and began to question whether he was still on the bed. He could no longer distinguish where his old human body ended and his new puppy one began.

"She's going to leave me," Robert sobbed. "I know she's going to leave me."

Robert fell into silence for several seconds before yelling more loudly than he had all day: *"Why does everybody always leave me?!"*

Don couldn't control himself anymore and began violently convulsing on the bed. His paws scratched at the sheets until he heard the comforter and pillows fall to the floor. He felt Robert whisk him to another part of his body—this time to the lungs.

"Why does everybody always leave me?" Robert cried.

Don could only hear every other word as Robert struggled for air between hiccups.

"My . . . mother . . . left . . . me," Robert gasped. "My . . . father . . . left . . . me."

Don logically knew that both of his parents had died from a disease they couldn't control, but he had always felt in his heart that they intentionally left him because he wasn't a good baby.

"Why . . . did . . . they . . . leave . . . me?

"What . . . did . . . I . . . do . . . wrong?

"Why . . . did . . . she . . . hate . . . me?

"Mommies . . . aren't . . . supposed . . . to hate . . . their . . . babies!"

Don felt more anger in his soul than he ever had in his life. There was something profoundly liberating about feeling his emotions outwardly expressed, and he began to regret not doing it more often.

After lying still for several minutes, Don noticed that the pain in his old abdomen was significantly less intense than it had been before. His entire torso seemed several pounds lighter, and the darkness that had engulfed his pancreas was also much lighter. The pain was definitely still present, but it was many degrees less pervasive than it had been before.

"Is it gone?" asked Don.

"Is what gone?"

"The cancer."

"Not completely," replied Robert. "But it's mostly dislodged from the organs, and it should be a lot easier to expel now that it's moving around freely."

Don was exhausted as he felt Robert guide him back into his puppy body. However, when he returned, there was one thing he couldn't stop himself from thinking about. "Am I a horrible person because I was angry at my mother for dying?"

"Of course not—it's just what you felt, that's

all. It's perfectly natural to feel angry when a parent dies."

"Because logically she couldn't have *intended* to die, right?"

Robert remained silent.

"Right?" repeated Don.

"Anything's possible," Robert replied cryptically. "But now it's time for you to return to your *new* mother."

Robert carried him into the garage, and quietly set him down next to his puppy siblings. Don felt comforted by his new family, which seemed remarkably less complicated than the memories of his human one.

CHAPTER NINE

"Why are you ignoring me?" Suzanne asked after yet another meal of sliced fruit and French bread.

"I'm not ignoring you," Robert said. "I just don't have anything to say."

"It's not what you say; it's how you're acting."

"I'm fine." He looked up briefly from his food and smiled.

"You're not fine. *We're* not fine. You're always ignoring me."

"I'm *not* ignoring you." He raised his voice slightly. "I'm just focusing all my energy on recovering right now."

Suzanne *was* thankful he was concentrating on recovering. Less than a month ago, she had been positive that her husband had given up his will to live and was on the way out. It was true that a remarkable shift had taken place where he was genuinely trying to get better, and it seemed to be working. However, it was also becoming increasingly difficult to ignore the fact that his personality was changing as well. Before, she had been his whole life, almost to the point of his smothering her at times. But now she felt like he didn't care if she was around or not—it was as if they had become roommates.

"I just feel lonely, that's all," Suzanne said quietly.

"That's why we got you a dog," Robert said flippantly.

Her husband's words felt like a slap in the face. "Why would you say such a thing?"

"You heard the doctor," replied Robert. "There isn't any hope for me recovering completely. It's just a matter of time."

"But you're getting so much better. Maybe we should go to the doctor and see if it's in remission."

"There's no point," Robert said. "We both know

it's a waste of money. Let's just enjoy one day at a time."

Suzanne had been trying to do just that, but with her husband's remarkable recovery, she started to let herself hope that the cancer would somehow go away.

They both sat in the dining room without speaking—the clinking sounds of silverware on plates filling the uncomfortable silence. After several minutes, Suzanne reached over to caress her husband's scruffy face, and he quickly pulled away from her.

"When are you going to shave?" she asked.

"I'm not going to," he said matter-of-factly.

"Why not?" She was genuinely surprised by his answer. Until recently, he had shaved every day since she'd known him. "Doesn't it bug you?"

"No, it feels good. Much more natural than scraping my hair off every day."

"I'm going to bed," Suzanne sighed. "Are you coming?"

"No, I'm going to visit the puppies. I'll be in shortly."

"I was thinking," said Don, "maybe I should stay here."

Don had gotten used to communicating with Robert telepathically, and it was becoming second nature. It was only slightly different from when they were both in the same body, yet their connection was still remarkably strong.

"You can't stay here, Don. Our souls made an agreement."

"But . . . maybe I should stay so I can take care of Suzanne."

"I hate to break it to you, but you're a dog now. Suzanne needs a human to take care of her."

"But I can love her."

"You already have. Now it's someone else's turn."

The thought of Suzanne with someone else made Don much angrier than he had thought it would, and he tried his best to focus instead on the love he received from his new mother. Sadie was incredibly nurturing, and he felt safe and happy for the first time in years. "I like it here," Don finally said.

"Suzanne can't keep nine dogs anyway. She's probably going to give most of the puppies away in the next few weeks while they're still cute."

That saddened Don immensely. There was an intense bond between all of his puppy siblings, and he couldn't imagine them being split up. "Maybe someone would want all of us?"

"Not likely. Come on, Don—I know your new instincts are difficult to ignore, but you're going to have to accept your destiny. You're no longer a human, and you aren't entirely a dog either. You've been saved from having to learn all your life lessons over again, but from here on out you're going to need to trust me. When I say we have to leave, we have to leave. We're inexorably tied together for the rest of this lifetime, and like it or not, I have a lot to do here. So say your goodbyes and get ready to go."

Don closed his eyes as tightly as possible and grunted.

"Okay?" Robert asked.

Don curled into a furry ball and pretended to be asleep.

"Come on, let's go," Robert said aloud.

Don whimpered sheepishly. "Can I say goodbye to Suzanne?"

"It's not possible; she's already asleep." Robert was growing impatient.

"Can't I at least *look* at her one more time?" Don's eyes had finally opened a few days earlier.

"Oh, all right"—Robert sighed—"but you have to be quiet."

Robert picked up the small puppy and quietly walked through the house to the bedroom door. When they arrived, he gestured for Don to be silent by placing his index finger to his lips, and the puppy nodded. Slowly he opened the door, and they saw Suzanne lying in the bed, her long hair spread out on the pillow and her soft lips slightly parted to allow deep breaths to escape through her mouth. Don remembered the first time they had spent the night together: he had watched her sleep all night, enamored with how her hidden night beauty had revealed itself when she began to dream.

When they first started dating, they would often joke about visiting each other in their dreams. In light of recent events, Don was inclined to believe it had actually happened, and he decided to try it one last time.

He closed his eyes and concentrated as hard as he could. Through the darkness he saw a young Suzanne appear, being pushed on a merry-go-round in a small-town park. She had shown him a photo of this place many times before, as it reminded her of her dad. Don stood next to Suzanne's father in the park and watched her spin around, her ponytails bobbing up and down as she held tightly to the galvanized-metal rails. He thought he saw a glance of recognition directed at him while she quickly spun around. Her eyes became a window to their future, and he saw their entire life together flash before him in an instant.

Gradually, the park began to fade, and Don found himself standing in darkness. He felt Robert nudge him, and when he opened his eyes, he saw the clock glowing 11:11 on the nightstand next to his wife's pillow.

"Ready?" Robert asked telepathically.

After Don nodded, they slowly backed out of the room, and Robert quietly closed the door behind them.

Robert carried him outside through the garage door and walked down the pathway to the rusted off-white Land Cruiser parked in front of the house.

"This one, right?" he asked the puppy as he opened the squeaky passenger door.

Don responded by jumping out of Robert's arms and onto the ripped upholstered passenger seat. Don loved his Land Cruiser. It was the first car he had bought when he graduated from college, and it was built like a tank. He seldom made full use of the four-wheel drive, but even on city streets it gave him a feeling of invincibility that he lacked when he wasn't behind the wheel.

Robert got in on the driver's side, started the engine, and turned on the headlights. He sat motionless with his hands on the wheel and closed his eyes tightly.

"Haven't you ever driven a stick?" asked Don.

Robert pushed the leftmost pedal to the floorboard and used both hands to force the gearshift into first. He looked at the puppy quizzically and shrugged his shoulders.

"The parking brake!" Don found it hard to contain his frustration. He'd never let anyone drive his car before, and it didn't seem like Robert knew how to drive at all.

"Oh, right." Robert released the lever and let out the clutch. The Land Cruiser surged forward and threw the small puppy to the back of the seat. After nearly half a block of stopping and starting, Robert appeared to get the hang of it, and they slowly rolled past the stop sign at the end of their street.

"Stop sign! . . . Do you want me to drive?" Don asked without thinking.

They simultaneously burst into laughter and

continued to chuckle through the winding streets until they reached the highway. After about ten minutes, they merged onto Interstate 5.

"Where are we going?" asked Don.

"First we're going to take care of your legacy, then on to our destiny." Robert laughed.

"My legacy? What does that mean?"

"You wanted to die, right? So the first thing we need to do is make sure everyone thinks that's exactly what happened."

"How are we going to do that?"

"Don't worry; you're not actually going to die. We're just going to make it look that way."

"Is that really necessary?"

"Isn't that sweet?" Robert laughed. "Three weeks as a dog, and you've already rediscovered your will to live."

"Very funny." Don wasn't amused. "I'm just worried it will crush Suzanne. Maybe I can just disappear."

"Suzanne is the main reason you need to die— or at least appear to. She's going to need closure, and the most compassionate thing you can do is give her the opportunity to move on as quickly as possible. And besides, she'll find your letter first thing tomorrow morning."

"You left the letter I wrote?"

"Yep, it's on her desk chair."

Don had forgotten about the suicide note. "Why did you do that?"

"I *told* you why I did it—Suzanne needs closure. It's not like you have a choice anyway. Do you really think she's going to stay married to a dog?"

"Why are you such a jerk sometimes?"

"Come on, Don, we're going to have a great time. Just think of this as the beginning of your next adventure."

Don curled up in a ball on the ripped car seat and closed his eyes. He started to get depressed and wondered if he should have killed himself when he still had a chance. In some ways he felt as if he were being played like a puppet by Robert and was no longer in control of his own life.

They continued heading south on the freeway through central Oregon. The night was clear, and the full moon illuminated the road with an other-worldly silver light. There were very few other vehicles on the freeway, just an occasional logging truck that appeared to be bringing raw lumber to California. After a couple of hours, they came to a series of mountain passes that challenged both the Land Cruiser and Robert's driving ability.

"Slow down!" Don said after he was thrust against the passenger door when Robert took a curve too quickly. "This isn't a sports car—it has a much higher center of gravity. You need to take it easy!"

"But the engine seemed like it was going to die when I slowed down."

"You have to shift into second gear."

Robert attempted to downshift without pressing the clutch pedal, and the transmission made a horrible grinding sound.

"The clutch!" Don said telepathically while letting out a very puppylike yelp.

Robert quickly depressed the clutch and down-shifted. "Thanks, I forgot."

Ascending the mountains was slow going in second gear, and several logging trucks passed them on the winding two-lane freeway. They continued to make their way through the mountains, and after nearly half an hour of winding through the passes, a road sign caught Robert's attention.

"Merlin! That sounds interesting. Have you ever been to Merlin?"

"Nope," said Don. "Never been."

"Well, tonight's your lucky night," Robert said as he took the next exit. "We're going to Merlin to conclude your legacy."

Don sat up to see outside the passenger window as they approached Merlin. There wasn't a town center to speak of, and within just a few minutes the sporadic houses and occasional mini-mall had been replaced by a densely populated forest of tall evergreens.

"Is that it?" Don asked. "My legacy is going to conclude in the middle of some random forest?"

"Be patient. I feel something calling us farther up the road."

They continued to wind through the pitch-black forest, which was illuminated by their headlights and an occasional moonbeam. After about fifteen minutes, they approached another sign that caught Robert's attention.

"'Hellgate Canyon,'" Robert read the sign aloud. "This must be it."

"That sounds ominous—I don't know if I like that."

Robert swerved off the road to the widened dirt viewing area. As soon as they rolled to a dusty stop, he unbuckled his seat belt and jumped down from the Land Cruiser. He quickly walked around and opened the passenger door for Don. The puppy stared at him without moving before Robert picked him up and gently placed him down on the ground.

Suzanne had regularly complained about how tall the Land Cruiser was after Don put the extra-large wheels on, and even refused to ride in it after she had a very unladylike experience exiting it while wearing a dress. Don always liked how high the small vehicle was—it made him feel safe since he could see above all the cars in front of him. But in his new form, he wasn't sure if he still liked it as much.

"I don't see anything," said Don. "Are you sure this is the right place?"

"Follow me." Robert led the puppy several steps to the edge of a steep cliff overlooking the canyon below. The full moon illuminated the sharp rock edges, and its reflection shimmered on the water below that flowed into three distinct pools connected by a sinewy river. As they approached the edge of the cliff, Don got vertigo and instinctively took a step back in order to soak in the moonlit beauty from a safer distance.

"I feel weird," Don said plainly.

"The energy here is intense. There's a lot of history trapped in these boulders. Many dreams have been crushed, and several people have lost their lives here. Their spirits remain, and some still aren't sure what happened to them."

"How did they die?"

"I'm not sure—mostly tragic accidents, I think. Drowning, perhaps."

"I don't like it here."

Robert walked around the edge of the knee-high rock wall and came to a bouquet of wilted flowers next to a small photograph of a teenage girl that was encased in a plastic bag. "Look at this," he said. "I think it's some sort of memorial. It looks like Sarah took this corner a little too fast."

Don joined Robert next to the makeshift memorial. He glanced at the flowers briefly and noticed tiny shards of glass and reflective plastic that glimmered on the ground nearby. "You're morbid," he said. "Do you get pleasure out of all this? I want to go—let's leave."

"There's nothing morbid about death. It's as natural as breathing. But what's sad is that Sarah doesn't know she's no longer living on this plane. She's still here, and she's confused. I suppose I should help—we don't have much time left tonight, but I *did* take the oath."

"What oath?"

"The Oath of the Psychopomp," Robert said matter-of-factly.

"Psychopomp? What's a psychopomp?"

"It's someone who helps souls transition to the other side after they have died. It's a tradition that used to be very common, but over time the funeral ritual has all but destroyed it in Western cultures."

"I thought that's what a funeral was for."

"No, a funeral is for the living only. But the deceased are the ones who really need the help—especially if they die suddenly in an accident, like Sarah here."

"So what are you going to do?"

"I'm going to perform a short ritual. If you were still in human form, I'd ask you to do the posture with me, but you can still join me in the soundings."

"Soundings? But my voice isn't—"

"It's okay," Robert interrupted. "Your voice will be fine. Just listen to me, and mimic what I'm doing the best you can. It's not the sound itself, but the intent. What we're going to do is open a path to the afterlife that will be easy for Sarah to follow. Are you ready?"

"I guess so."

Robert carefully aligned himself so the memorial was between him and the full moon above. His feet were spaced about six inches apart, and he deliberately brought his hands to the sides of his head and placed them gently above his ears with his palms covering his temples. His arms were bowed out on either side to make the shape of a large circle. Slowly he hinged his neck back as far as it would go and opened his mouth wide. He stayed still in that posture for several seconds and, without warning, began to let out a strange, eerie sound.

"Ahhhhhhh . . ." he started quietly and carried the sound for nearly fifteen seconds before stopping. The canyon walls echoed his voice ominously like a huge outdoor cathedral for nearly as long as it had taken him to utter the first verse. Robert then took a deep breath and repeated louder: "Ahhhhhhh . . ."

Robert and the canyon continued their duet for several minutes before Don was ready to join in. Ever since he had first tried to speak in the garage, Don had felt self-conscious about his new voice and had spent most of his time as a puppy in silence. At first he tried to mimic Robert, but all that came out was a squeaky whimper. He then remembered what Robert had said about intent and decided to try making a sound while filling his heart with the word *go*.

Go, he thought over and over. *Go*. He then opened his puppy mouth wide, and out came a loud, high-pitched howl unlike any sound he had ever made before. It was simultaneously piercing and soulful and made him feel powerful and confident.

Don's howl entwined with Robert's voice perfectly, and the canyon joined in by echoing their two voices. They continued ahhing and howling, with both the intensity and volume compounding with every verse. After the fifth time, Don thought he could see a faint glow coming out of his mouth whenever he began to howl. It looked as if the mist from his mouth was reflecting the moonbeams; however, it wasn't cold enough outside for his breath to mist. He thought he was imagining it at first, until he looked over to Robert and saw that he, too, had a faint glow coming out of his mouth. The glow seemed to get brighter and more pronounced with every howl, and it began to travel through the night sky toward a shining star that appeared to simultaneously draw closer to Earth.

After several minutes of howling, the light beam remained fully illuminated and seemed to connect the cliff they were standing on to the star above, which by then appeared nearly close enough to touch. Robert gestured with his hand to be silent, and they both stood perfectly still as they let the echoes of their voices wash over the canyon walls. Don watched the light beam sparkle and dance as if it was alive and waiting for someone to join its graceful path.

As soon as the echoes fell to silence nearly a full minute later, Don instinctively inhaled a huge breath and let out the loudest, most piercing howl he could muster. "Ahhhhhhhhhhh!" they howled together, and almost immediately, Don could see the soul of the young girl float slowly toward the light beam. The vaguely humanlike shape had an amorphous borealis-like glow that shimmered with an otherworldly quality that was undeniably . . . *alive.*

As soon as she connected to the glimmering light, a brilliant flash traveled quickly and deliberately up the beam and to the star above. The entire sky flashed white, as if a massive lightbulb had been switched on, and just as quickly was gone. The light beam and the star overhead had disappeared in an instant, and the night returned to darkness. And although the full moon was still present, it appeared remarkably dim compared to the brilliant star that was no longer around.

Don fell to the ground and closed his eyes while panting loudly.

"That was intense," he said after he caught his breath. "Is she gone now?"

"Yes, she's finally where she needs to be."

"Do you do that a lot?"

"Not so much anymore," Robert laughed. "I used to, but now I try to avoid situations where unexpected deaths are a certainty."

"What do you mean?"

"Once I spent an entire lifetime helping thousands of people who didn't know they were dead transition to the other side." His tone became very serious. "You have never seen so much confusion and angst in all of your life—it was utterly horrendous. I never want to see that again."

"Where was that?"

Robert remained silent for several seconds. In the moonlight, Don could see a look of complete and absolute horror overtake his face.

"Hiroshima," Robert finally said in a quiet, shaky voice. "1945."

They sat in silence for several minutes, and Don began to feel sorry for Robert. He couldn't imagine how it must have felt to see thousands of disembodied souls that didn't understand why they were instantly killed. War was the worst thing he could imagine, but he had never thought about what happened to the souls *after* they died.

Ever since Don had met Robert, his perspective on how he viewed himself and others had changed dramatically. Before, he believed that he and his body were one and the same. But now he was living inside the body of a dog, and his new friend was living inside the body he used to call his own. It was all very confusing, and he began to wish for a simpler time when dead people were dead and living people were living, and never the two should meet.

"Okay, enough of this sad talk." Robert laughed and stood up while brushing the dust from his pants. "Come on now, we have a death to fake."

Robert hopped over the stone wall and disappeared into the darkness. Don could hear his friend rummaging through the brush, and in less than a minute, Robert reappeared with two medium-sized twisted branches. Don recognized the smooth red bark of the manzanita bush, which was one of his favorites.

"What are you going to do with those?" he asked.

Robert ignored the question and deliberately walked to the car and tossed the branches onto the passenger seat. Don followed him and watched while he started up the Land Cruiser and slowly backed it into the middle of the road. After it was positioned, Robert switched the lights on, which shone brightly onto the rock wall that divided the road from the canyon below.

He then got out and used the first branch to depress the clutch, and kept it in place by positioning the other end against the ripped vinyl seat. He climbed back in and shifted the transmission into the lowest gear. After getting out, he deliberately positioned the second branch against the gas pedal, which instantly revved the engine to a high-pitched whine.

When Don finally realized what was happening, he ran up to Robert and instinctively tugged his pant leg with his puppy teeth. "What are you doing to my car?! Isn't there another way?"

"Get out of the way," yelled Robert over the loud engine. "You don't need this car anymore, and this is the perfect way for Suzanne to get closure. Don't be selfish—it's not about you."

These words hit Don hard. He ran through the different options in his mind and couldn't think of anything better. As he was reflecting on Suzanne, he saw Robert empty his pockets and throw Don's wallet onto the front seat before dramatically pulling away the branch that was depressing the clutch. The Land Cruiser surged into gear and sped toward the rock wall.

Through Don's eyes, everything appeared in slow motion as the large tires of the four-wheel-drive automobile connected with the hand-laid masonry. He thought he saw the vehicle bounce back for an instant, and then it heaved forward as the deep tread gripped the top of the barrier and pulled the front wheels up and over the wall.

At that moment, everything sped back into real time, and the back wheels effortlessly scaled the wall and the car appeared to glide down the cliff and into the canyon below. About halfway down, it flipped over and continued to cartwheel down the massive boulders until it plunged into the river with a huge splash. The engine was instantly silenced, and other than the sound of rocks and pebbles sliding down the mountain, the air in the majestic canyon was calm once again.

"There," Robert said dryly. "You're dead. Let's get going before someone comes to find out what just happened."

Don was stunned as he watched the Land Cruiser being swallowed by the water below. When the last wheel sank out of sight, his mind turned to Suzanne, and he realized he would never see her again. He was intensely disappointed in himself that he had been the one to leave her. His entire life was filled with the pain and suffering from his parents' leaving *him* at such an early age. And he had ended up abandoning the only person he'd ever loved. He had always felt that Suzanne was going to eventually leave him, but in the end he left *her*—and he could never forgive himself for doing so.

But even more disturbing was how out of control he felt. Robert had completely taken over his life, and it didn't seem to matter what *he* wanted anymore. Don wondered if he had made the right decision and started to regret not killing himself when he had the opportunity. It was probably still possible to commit suicide as a dog, but he didn't know how to do it.

"Come on," urged Robert. "Let's go."

Don begrudgingly followed Robert after looking at his car once more. He saw the last part of the bumper sticking out of the water and the moon reflecting on the river as if nothing had happened.

The two of them walked in silence along the winding forest road, illuminated by the moonbeams filtered through the tall conifers. After walking nearly two hours without a word, they came to a long, narrow wood building with striped canvas drapes pulled along its entire length. Scattered throughout the yard were various pieces of furniture, including a large, overstuffed love seat. They instinctively drifted through the split-rail fence and stood in front of the love seat. Reflected in the moonlight at the top of the building was a hand-painted sign that read: MAXIMUM STAY IN THIS REST AREA 18 HOURS.

"Not a problem." Robert chuckled softly as he collapsed into the chair, stirring up a cloud of dust. Don jumped into his lap, and they both fell asleep instantly—exhausted from their long and eventful night.

CHAPTER TEN

n the morning, Suzanne was awakened by a loud knock at the front door. She was alone, since her husband once again hadn't come to bed. She thought that he had likely fallen asleep in the garage, as he had a habit of doing lately. The knocking continued, this time louder and more insistent.

"I'm coming," Suzanne said as she fumbled to find her robe. "I'll be right there."

Bleary-eyed, she opened the door to reveal two police officers standing on her doorstep. They both looked identical except that the female one had slightly longer hair.

"Can I help you?" asked Suzanne.

"Mrs. Newport?" replied the female cop in a plaintive voice.

"Yes?"

"I'm sorry, ma'am, but your husband's vehicle was involved in an accident last night."

"That's impossible," Suzanne replied. "His car is right . . ." Her words trailed off as she pointed to the street where the Land Cruiser had been parked for the past several weeks. However, the police car was in its place. "Oh my god," she gasped.

Suzanne left the officers on the front porch as she rushed into the garage, shouting her husband's name repeatedly. "Don!" she called out as she hurried from one room to the next. "This isn't funny! Where are you?"

After exploring every room of their small house three times, she returned to the porch, where the officers were patiently waiting. She was out of breath and visibly distraught.

"Where is he?" she asked. "Where is he now?"

"I'm sorry, ma'am, but we're not exactly sure at the moment."

"What do you mean you aren't exactly sure?! You said you found his car. What's going on here?" Suzanne began to hyperventilate. "Tell me what's going on!"

"Please calm down, ma'am. We want to tell you what we know."

Suzanne saw Don's wallet in the male officer's hand, and she instinctively grabbed for it. He handed her the damp leather wallet and spoke for the first time: "The vehicle was found at the bottom of a steep ravine, where it was submerged in water. This wallet washed up on the shore about a quarter mile downriver. We're still looking for your husband, but he would have found himself in some of the most treacherous waters in all of the Rogue River. "

Suzanne grew dizzy, and the light began to dim. She grabbed on to the doorjamb, trying to steady herself, before collapsing to the floor. Seated in the doorway, she thumbed through the wallet and found Don's driver's license. The photo was from several years ago when he still looked like he had when they'd first met. It was long before the cancer or financial problems, when life was much easier. There was also a photo of them together, which separated from its sodden backing as she removed it from the wallet.

"Are you sure?" Suzanne asked as she looked up to the officers.

"I'm afraid so, ma'am," the female cop replied. "I'm so sorry."

"What do I do now?"

"There's nothing you can do at the moment. We're attempting to remove the vehicle from the river as soon as possible, and we've already started a full-scale search and rescue to retrieve him. It's possible that your husband is still alive, and we're going to do everything we can to find him."

"It's 'possible' that he's still alive?" Uncharacteristically, Suzanne raised her voice. "*Possible?!*"

"Sorry, ma'am. We're going to do everything we can to find him."

"You already said that." Suzanne was getting annoyed with their by-the-book answers.

"I apologize, ma'am. I understand this is a very difficult situation for you."

"Did you see the car?"

The male cop nodded. "We just drove from the scene directly here," he said, averting his eyes. "Is there someone we can call for you, ma'am?"

Suzanne shook her head as the cops began to fade out of focus.

"It's helpful if a friend or family member can be with you right now."

"No." Suzanne continued to shake her head. "I want to be alone."

Apparently on cue, both officers handed Suzanne

their business cards and said in unison, "These are our numbers."

The female added, "Call if you have any questions or if there's anything we can do to help. I've also written the number of Social Services on the back of my card. Give them a call if you need someone to talk to."

Suzanne pulled herself back up to a standing position and took the cards. "Okay, thank you," she said in a scratchy voice and mindlessly shut the door in their faces.

"Oh my god," she said as she stumbled toward the kitchen. "Oh my god."

As she came to her yellow desk, she noticed an envelope on her chair that was inscribed with the words *Dearest Suzanne*. She immediately picked it up and ripped it open to reveal a letter that was written in her husband's handwriting:

> *Dearest Suzanne,*
>
> *I'm so sorry to leave you. You are the love of my life, and I am forever indebted to you for all you have done for me. But I can no longer go on. The pain, the money, the stress . . . it's just not worth it. I was going to be gone anyway before the end of the year. Please don't be mad at me for leaving on my own terms.*

Don't grieve for me, and do whatever you need to do without me. Your happiness is all that matters.

Thank you for a beautiful life.
Your husband, Don

Suzanne's tears began to dot the letter she was holding as her hands shook uncontrollably. Her stomach wrenched in knots, and she could barely catch her breath before she let out a piercing scream that rattled the glassware.

"Damn you!" she yelled at the top of her lungs. "You selfish brat—damn you! How could you do this to me?"

Suzanne ripped the letter in half. And then she ripped it in half again. She kept tearing it into smaller and smaller pieces until the letter was an unrecognizable pile of confetti. She then shoved the handful of tiny papers into her mouth and began chewing. She nearly gagged when she tried to swallow the pulpy mess. "Damn you!" she screamed again, and her eyes rolled to the back of her head as she fell to the floor and lost consciousness.

CHAPTER ELEVEN

"I wonder if the puppy comes with this chair," joked Peter.

"Yeah, and we could use an extra hippie around the house." Miranda giggled.

Don opened his eyes and saw two figures standing in front of the rising sun: a tall, balding man with thick glasses next to a short, curly-haired redheaded woman wearing a bright yellow sundress. The corners of their eyes and mouths proudly displayed many years of deep lines and wrinkles, revealing that they both laughed easily.

"Good morning," Peter laughed. "I'm Peter, and this is Miranda—we're pleased to make your acquaintance."

"Nice to meet you—I'm Robert, and this is Don," Robert said while gesturing to the puppy.

"When does this place open?" asked Peter.

Don looked around to remind himself of where they had spent the night. Everything came back to him as he read the large sign at the top of the building that said: ANTIQUES.

"It says it's closed Sundays," yelled Miranda, who had crossed the parking lot to look at the store more closely. "I guess we're out of luck."

Peter shrugged and said, "Oh well. I guess we don't need any more furniture anyway. So what are you doing here, Robert? Why are you sleeping in the parking lot?"

"Our car . . . died," said Robert. "Just trying to figure out what to do next."

At that moment, two police cars sped toward Hellgate Canyon with their sirens blaring loudly.

"Where are you from?" Robert raised his voice over the sound of the sirens.

Miranda rejoined Peter and responded, "We're from Portland. You?"

"Eugene," replied Robert, and with that, Don whimpered softly. Hearing Robert say the name of his hometown was strangely disturbing.

"We like Eugene," said Miranda. "We go to the Oregon Country Fair every year."

In all the years he had lived there, Don had only been to the Country Fair twice. Both times he went with Suzanne, and although they had enjoyed it, they began to resent all the hippies who took over Eugene once a year.

"Where are you headed?" asked Peter.

"South," Robert said after a long pause.

"When's your car going to be fixed?"

"It's beyond repair," Robert laughed. "We just left a note to have it towed to the nearest junkyard."

"That's too bad," said Peter.

"Maybe we should see Hellgate Canyon before we leave," Miranda changed the subject.

"It's not very interesting," interjected Robert. "We were there yesterday—it's just a bunch of rocks and trees. We were quite disappointed."

Peter and Miranda walked toward their car while talking to each other discreetly. After several seconds of whispering, Peter stepped forward and announced, "We can give you a ride as far as Ashland if you want."

"That would be great," replied Robert. "When are you leaving?"

"I guess soon. Other than Hellgate Canyon, this was the only place left we wanted to see. And with your glowing review, I guess we don't need to go there." Peter laughed again and winked at Miranda.

"I'm ready to go. Are you ready, dear?"

"Sure," Miranda responded. "How about you two?"

"Absolutely," said Robert. "Let's get out of here."

The four of them got into the couple's silver sedan, and they started heading back toward the freeway. Peter was driving and Miranda sat in the front passenger seat. Robert and Don were in the backseat, scrunched between a pile of suitcases and duffle bags.

"Sorry about the room back there," said Miranda. "We're going for a weeklong retreat in Ashland, and then we'll be heading down to Mount Shasta for a week after that. Two weeks of clothes is a lot to pack."

Robert nodded.

"Oh dear, where's *your* luggage?" Miranda asked. "Did we leave it back at the antique store?"

"No," said Robert. "We're traveling light. We'll pick something up when we settle somewhere."

"Oh. That's the best way. If I could buy new clothes in every town we went to, I definitely would."

"Miranda *loves* clothes." Peter laughed loudly for several seconds.

"Which retreat are you two going to?" asked Robert.

"It's absolutely fascinating—we're going to an embodiment retreat," Miranda answered.

"Embodiment? What's that?"

"It's rather involved, but the short answer is that it's about being fully in your body so you can live a more authentic life."

"Most people leave their bodies whenever things get difficult," added Peter.

"Yes, that's true—trauma, abuse, that sort of thing," continued Miranda, turning around in her seat so she could face her passengers. "For example, when you experience severe emotional stress, you have a built-in defense mechanism that allows you to temporarily leave your body, or shut down a part of yourself, to give you a break from the pain. And after years of doing this, many of us get used to living outside our bodies because it seems to be easier to remain disconnected from ourselves than to stay connected with each of the three *spirit bodies* that are designed to live inside of us."

"This is important," Robert said to Don telepathically. *"I'm familiar with what she's talking about, and I think this will help you a lot. Let me know if you have any questions, and I'll ask her for you."*

"Spirit *bodies?*" asked Robert for Don's benefit. "There are more than one?"

"Yes, our *soul* is made up of three spirit bodies that all work together. They are our *spirit of awareness, spirit of emotion,* and *spirit of physical sensation.*"

"Okay . . ."

"And when these three spirit bodies are fully activated within our soul, we naturally integrate fully with our *human body,* and that's what we call *embodiment.*"

"Could you explain more about the three spirit bodies?" Robert again voiced Don's question.

"Of course. Awareness is the part of us that is conscious of ourselves and the world around us. It allows us to learn and remember things that make our lives easier and more productive. Many of us can relate to our spirit of awareness through our mental capacity."

"You mean awareness is *thinking?*"

"That's part of it, but it includes spiritual awareness as well. It is about knowing on all levels, not just intellectually. Do you understand?"

"I think so," Robert said while looking at Don. "Tell me about the other two qualities."

"Sure. Emotion is the most complex of the three spirit bodies, even though it has the clearest of jobs. Basically, emotions are simply for our protection and nothing else. And in order to accomplish such a noble goal, they are in perpetual motion, attempting to balance the signals they are sending to us by constantly counteracting themselves with even *more* emotions."

"Emotions are for protection. How does that work?"

"It's simple if you think about it. Let's say a car is coming right at you while you're walking across the street. Your emotions will release *fear* to get you to jump out of the way. Now the problem we have is that we can easily get too much of a good thing—a little goes a long way. For example, if we get addicted to an emotion like fear, it can easily debilitate us and prevent us from doing anything productive. And although fear is a wonderful emotion, too much can be quite traumatizing."

"No wonder people want to deaden their emotions. It seems exhausting to be in a constant balancing act."

"When there is a need to be protected, our emotions are in constant motion. However, when we are still, our emotions are still, also. The beauty is that all of them come from a single emotion— *love.* And when we stay connected to our emotions, we are filled with love throughout our entire being. It's that love that makes us feel safe, content, and happy."

"But why do you say that our 'physical sensation' is a part of our soul? Most spiritual practices teach us that we should become detached from our physical body. In fact, that's the very goal of many of them. Isn't our physical sensation obviously part of our physical *body?*"

"Our soul is the part of us that's *infinitely* alive. The human body, the part that you and I see, is simply a container for our spirit and is only alive in a very limited way. And although the human body obviously has receptors in it—for example, taste buds—the sensation itself is felt by our soul. And when there's a disconnect between the two, that's when things can happen to our human body that we can't actually feel."

"You mean when we go into shock after severe pain?"

"Yes, that's a good example."

"So what's the point of having physical sensation from a spiritual perspective? It seems pointless."

"Ah, but it's not. Physical sensation gives us pleasure, and that pleasure gives us motivation to live a fulfilling life here on Earth. Whether it's feeling a caress on our cheek, eating a delicious meal, or listening to a beautiful song, our physical sensations are the gifts the universe gives us in order to stay motivated to continue our work. Therefore, when we deaden our physical sensation, we become depressed because we are no longer rewarded for being here. And unfortunately, that's something I know *a lot* about."

"It sounds like you know a lot about *all* this stuff," said Robert. "How do you know so much about embodiment if you haven't been to the retreat yet?"

"We've been before. Next week is level-two teacher training—we've already completed level one."

"And what got you interested in this work?"

"The same thing that motivates most therapists: I was severely damaged and wanted to heal myself—"

"That's an understatement," interrupted Peter.

"I was physically abused as a little girl," continued Miranda. "After nearly forty years of depression—and fifteen as a practicing psychotherapist—this work helped me realize that one of my biggest problems was that I had cut myself off from my physical sensation many years ago."

"How did you realize that?" Robert asked.

"From the embodiment exercises. I can show you one if you want—we can do it here in the car."

"Can Don do it, too?"

"I've never led a dog through the work before," Miranda replied. "But it should be okay if he can understand me."

"Don't worry about that," said Robert. "He can definitely understand you."

"Okay," Miranda said, shrugging her shoulders. "Both of you sit up straight."

Don sat up on the seat and instantly became nervous about what would happen next. He trusted Robert, but wasn't sure about this other person. She seemed nice but a little too happy.

"First close your eyes and find the absolute center of your head. It will be between your ears, and between the forehead and the back of your head."

Don closed his eyes and tried to find the center, mentally rocking side to side within his head. After a while he noticed that he was physically moving as well.

"Be patient," Miranda whispered in a calming voice. "You will know you're getting close when you can see a bright light in your mind's eye. Just move to the precise center within the middle of your head."

Don began to see a light glowing in the darkness of his mind.

"Just move slowly until you become engulfed by the light."

At that very instant, Don connected to the light, and with an electric flash, its energy traveled down his spine and throughout his entire core. All of a sudden, he was acutely aware of himself, and it was almost as if he could think with his entire body.

"That's great!" Miranda exclaimed. "Do you feel that?"

Don was startled that Miranda could apparently sense what was going on in his head. He was just starting to get used to Robert invading his thoughts, but he wasn't sure if he could handle someone else knowing what went on in his inner world.

"Now stay grounded in your awareness," Miranda continued, "and begin to breathe into your head—into that very light that you're inside of right now. Breathe deeply through your nose, and let the nourishing breath travel from your lungs to your awareness in one graceful movement. Nourish your awareness with each breath."

Don was initially skeptical about the idea of breathing into anywhere but his lungs; however, he was surprised by how easy it was once he stopped thinking about it. By breathing very slowly and controlling his breath so it flowed in and out in a single continuous motion, he could direct it to the center of his head. With every inhale, the breath seemed to fill his head with energy, and with every exhale, the energy seemed to calm and settle without going away. After several breaths, he found it remarkably relaxing.

"Good," Miranda said after letting the silence settle around them. "It seems like both of you are very connected to your awareness. Your mental faculties are quite developed. Let's move on to your emotions."

Don tensed up and immediately lost the connection to his awareness. He never liked the word *emotions,* and he felt uncomfortable when Miranda said it.

"Keep your eyes closed, and concentrate on your emotional center, which is located in the middle of your chest beneath the center of your sternum. Concentrate on this area until you come to a pool of emotion, which will feel like pure love, bliss, or joy."

Don had a much more difficult time locating this area and mentally tried to move to different places in his chest to find it.

"Don, try shifting your concentration toward the back of your spine—you are too far forward. You're concentrating at least six inches in front of your body."

Don tried to concentrate farther toward the back of his spine but still couldn't connect to anything resembling emotion, let alone love or bliss. He was used to avoiding all of the sensations in his chest and abdomen because of the cancer. And even though he was in a new body, he was still unable to connect with it.

"That's it!" Miranda exclaimed. "Very good, Robert—you've connected with your emotional center. It's not as developed as your awareness, but if you continue to practice, you will be able to fill yourself with even more love."

Don was annoyed that Robert had connected with his emotions before *he* did. He knew it wasn't a competition, but there was something about Robert doing it first that irked him.

"Now, Don, you still need to move back farther. I know it seems scary, but being in your body is nothing to be afraid of. I understand there was a very good reason for you to disconnect from your emotions—I'm sure it was very painful. But now it's safe. Just relax and concentrate a few inches more toward the back of your spine."

Miranda's words had a calming effect on him— then he began to feel dizzy, as if he was moving backward and forward at the same time. When his movement came into focus, he felt a sensation like a warm liquid dripping slowly from the center of his chest and into his belly.

"There you go," Miranda said softly. "Doesn't that feel nice?"

Don was astonished by how comforted he felt. It was a feeling he hadn't experienced in many years, yet it surprised him how familiar it was.

"You both need to regularly practice connecting to your emotions," she continued. "It will become much easier the more you do. Are you ready to move on to your physical sensation?"

For some reason Don felt exhausted, and he wanted nothing more than to go to sleep.

"Okay, this is the last one. I know these exercises are difficult, but it's important to also connect to your physical sensation to balance yourselves."

Don grunted out loud to indicate he was worn-out. It was surprising how tiring it was to be *in* his body.

"Concentrate on the area about an inch and a half below your navel. This is the center of your physical sensation. But just like the other parts of your spirit body, it actually permeates your entire being. See if you can feel the energy of your physical sensation."

By this point, Don was familiar with the procedure and quickly focused his attention on the area beneath his navel. Immediately he began to get uncomfortable, and shortly after, Robert vocalized what they were both feeling.

"I feel . . . shy," Robert said after a long pause.

"Unfortunately, that's a pretty common reaction by people living in today's society. Our physical center is directly connected to our sexuality, and over the years we are taught to be embarrassed of our bodies—especially as it relates to sexuality."

Don began to squirm, and although he was starting to appreciate the value of these exercises, he really didn't like this one at all. "Embarrassed" was an understatement. Since his mother had died, he hadn't had any role models for how couples were supposed to show affection toward each other. And other than an occasional pat on the back, his father had seldom touched him. It had taken Don several years not to retreat whenever Suzanne approached him with a hug. But now his embarrassment was taken to an entirely new level—while he was concentrating on his physical sensation, he realized for the first time since he'd entered his new body that he was . . . naked.

"The good news," continued Miranda, "is that you're both feeling it. It will take some practice to be able to tune in to the pleasures of physical sensation without feeling guilty or embarrassed; but at least there doesn't seem to be any serious blockages like what *I* had to deal with. For the first several months of trying to tune in to my own physical sensation, I couldn't feel a thing. My childhood abuse disconnected me from the physical aspect of my spirit so completely that it took many sessions of concentrated embodiment therapy before I could feel it at all."

Don felt sorry for Miranda. He had gone through many trials in this lifetime, but thankfully he never had to deal with being physically abused as a child.

"Now I want you both to slowly open your eyes and continue to breathe deeply. See if you can remain integrated with your spirit body while your eyes are open."

Don gradually opened his eyes and felt an unusual sensation when Miranda and the inside of the car came into focus. It appeared as if everything was much farther away and the car was much larger.

"Everything seems far away now," Robert said aloud.

"That's because you are finally back in your bodies. You both were living several inches in front of them, which is quite common. But now you are much more integrated, which is why everything seems farther away."

When Don heard this, he turned his attention to Miranda and found that he couldn't focus on her face. As he relaxed, his focus returned, but so did his depth perception. Everything moved much closer to him, as it had been before, and he felt angry when he realized that he had already lost his grip on his own body.

"Don't worry," said Miranda. "It takes practice before you can live from within your body if you're used to living outside of it. But doing this exercise on a regular basis will help."

"I don't mean to interrupt," Peter cut in, "but we've just arrived in downtown Ashland."

Don had noticed that the car had slowed down considerably, but he hadn't looked out the window to see that they had exited the freeway until Peter's announcement. They all sat in silence as they looked at the idyllic town square with green awnings, large hanging flower baskets, and oblivious pedestrians crossing the street in front of cars every half block.

"Thank you so much for sharing with me," said Miranda. "I've never worked with animals before, and I'm surprised by how receptive Don was to the work."

"He's very special," said Robert while looking at the puppy.

"Yes, I can see that," Miranda continued. "That was so inspiring! The possibilities are endless—I'm so excited."

"Me, too," said Peter dryly while rolling his eyes. "I'm sure there's a *huge* market for interspecies therapy."

"Oh, be quiet, grumpy," said Miranda.

"Where do you want to be dropped off, Robert?" Peter asked while looking in the rearview mirror.

"They can come with us to Martika's, don't you think?" said Miranda. She turned to Robert and Don. "Our friend who runs the retreat center is very generous and I'm sure she would be happy to give you a meal before sending you on your way."

Don hadn't eaten anything since they left Eugene and he *was* starting to get hungry.

"That sounds wonderful," said Robert. "We'd love to meet your friend."

CHAPTER TWELVE

fter a short drive through town, Peter turned toward the hills and entered an enclave of large country estates. The well-manicured properties were host to an impressive diversity of farm animals, including sheep, horses, llamas, and chickens. At the base of the hill, they turned in to a graveled driveway and parked between two red barnlike buildings.

"This is Martika's," said Miranda as she exited the car and stretched by bending backward and facing the sky. "I'll go in and tell her you'll be staying for dinner."

"Only if it's not too much trouble," said Robert.

"I'm sure it will be fine," she said as she walked toward the side entrance of the large house. "I'll be right back."

While they were waiting for Miranda to return with her friend, Robert noticed there was an aspect of the energy of this place that felt very familiar. He had never been to southern Oregon before, but there was something recognizable about the way this particular property was landscaped. The energy flow was very distinct and reminded him of something buried deep within his past. Peter continued to make small talk, but Robert was so distracted that he began to nod at inappropriate moments.

Then, behind him, he could feel someone approaching—the person who was responsible for the energy he was feeling. When he turned around, he saw a short blonde woman with wavy hair and a soft, content smile. She was wearing a flowing white cotton dress and carrying a silver serving tray with four glasses of ice water.

"Robert, this is Martika," said Miranda. "Martika, Robert."

"Nice to meet you, Robert." Martika sneezed loudly and nearly dropped the tray of water glasses. "Will you be joining us for dinner?" she sniffled.

"If it's not too much trouble," Robert replied. He tried to appear calm, but he couldn't control his shaking hand, which rattled the serving tray while he removed a glass.

"Is the room ready?" asked Peter.

"Yes, dear. Do you remember where it is?" Martika sneezed again as politely as she could while still holding the tray.

"Of course," said Miranda. "We'll see you at dinner. Thanks, Martika!" She followed Peter up the stairs to the top floor of one of the barnlike buildings.

Martika looked around intently and asked Robert, "Do you have a dog?"

"Yes, a black Lab," Robert said as he pointed to Don, who was staring at Martika from the seat of the car.

"Oh, that explains it." She sneezed again. "I'm deathly allergic to dogs—I should probably go inside. You're welcome to stay for dinner, but unfortunately, I'm going to have to insist on your dog remaining outside. I've been allergic since I was a little girl, and if I'm not careful, my throat will close up and I'll need to spend the night in the hospital."

Martika returned to the house, sneezing three more times in the short distance between the driveway and the French doors that accessed the kitchen. Robert watched her go inside and then returned to the car, finding Don curled up on the floorboard, shaking violently.

"What's wrong?" asked Robert. "Are you okay?"

"It's her," Don whimpered as he gestured toward the house.

"Martika? What about her?" Robert knew Martika held significance in his own life, but was surprised that Don was also having such a strong reaction to her.

"She looks just like my mother."

"How is that possible? You said she died of cancer."

"That's what my father told me, but my aunt said that she left us right after I turned two. My aunt said my mother couldn't handle being a parent and abandoned us."

This is going to get complicated, Robert thought. *I'm going to need to do more research in the future before picking my next host body.*

"Ask if her name is really Mary," continued Don. "I'm sure it's her. I had a photograph of her that I carried with me every day until you threw my wallet into the river. And isn't it just perfect—my own mother is allergic to me! I finally find her after all these years, and she gets physically ill whenever she's within twenty feet of me."

"I'm sorry," Robert said in a caring voice. "Are you okay?"

"No, I'm not okay," Don replied angrily. "Why is this happening to me? What good is all of this? Is this a cruel joke? Are you really here to help me, or are you just here to torture me?"

"I had no idea she was your mother."

"You're supposed to know everything." Don's silent words were accompanied by high-pitched yelping, and even a passerby would have assumed the young puppy was in pain.

"No," said Robert firmly. "The *universe* knows everything, and *that* is what brought you here today. All I knew was that your destiny wasn't fulfilled yet, and I'm sure this is one of the big reasons why. You needed to know that your mother was still alive and confront the fact that she intentionally abandoned you."

"I knew it," Don said angrily. "I knew she didn't love me."

Robert sighed and caressed the side of Don's muzzle. "I'm sure that's not true. How can a mother not love a face like this?"

"That's not funny."

"You're right—sorry. Okay, let me go talk to her now, and we can figure out what to do about all of this later."

Don let out a soft whimper. "Are you going tell her about me?"

Robert took a deep breath and sighed loudly. "I promise I will get the conversation started."

He then walked across the pea-graveled drive-way and knocked on the white French doors to the kitchen. Martika let him in and returned to the stove, where she stirred a large pot of rice before replacing the lid.

"Can I get you some tea?" she asked while gesturing for him to sit on a bar stool next to the marble-topped island.

"No, thank you," replied Robert as he gazed deep into Martika's eyes.

The intensity seemed to take Martika by surprise, and she sat opposite him, trying to return his gaze while straightening up the counter. Her fidgeting eventually stopped, and they continued staring at each other for several seconds without saying a word. Robert could see that Martika's hands were shaking, and she self-consciously sat on her fingers as soon as she noticed he was watching.

"Martika," said Robert. "That's an interesting name."

"My given name is Mary, but that means 'bitter,'" she laughed nervously. "And I didn't want to be bitter my entire life, so I changed it."

"When was that?"

"Hmm, let me think. I guess it would be nearly thirty-seven years ago—wow, how time flies. It was on my eighteenth birthday. I needed to escape my old life, so I changed my name and left everything I knew behind."

"I see," Robert said knowingly.

"Do you know where you're staying?" Martika asked after an uncomfortable silence.

"Not yet. Don and I will probably sleep under the stars somewhere. It's getting warm, and it will be nice to wake up in nature again."

"Is Don your puppy?"

"I wouldn't say *my* puppy. But I have made an agreement to take care of him for a while." Robert laughed.

"Oh." Martika shifted in her seat uncomfortably. "I'm so sorry I can't invite him in, but I'm just so allergic."

"It's okay—I'm sure he'll eventually understand." Robert was trying to be funny, but as the words came out, he wasn't sure that Don *would* understand.

Robert again looked deep into Martika's eyes and held her gaze for as long as she would allow it. He could sense her profound sadness, which in turn made *him* feel melancholy. She clearly wasn't having an easy life this time around, and Robert felt sorry for her.

"I need to change my clothes before dinner." Martika nervously fidgeted with the vase in the center of the counter. "Do either of you have any dietary needs I should be aware of?"

"No, I'll eat anything—but Don doesn't like fruit."

"I'm guessing that most dogs don't," she laughed. "I'll see you in a bit."

During dinner, Martika played the role of the gracious host, single-handedly preparing and serving a delicious meal of asparagus risotto for the seven visitors who were staying on her property for the retreat. She dutifully made conversation with all of her guests, but was secretly nervous about talking to Robert and avoided him all night.

After dinner, the guests all went back to their rooms to get some rest for the first day of the retreat.

However, Robert stayed seated, and when everyone else was gone, he silently joined Martika in the kitchen to help her clean up.

Robert once again held her gaze with an intensity that Martika had never felt before. There was something profoundly familiar about the way he stared at her, a look that she had dreamed about several times throughout the years. She remembered searching many people's faces for these very eyes, but as the years progressed, she had let the dream fade and had all but forgotten about it until this moment.

"Do I know you?" Martika finally asked.

"Yes," Robert said matter-of-factly.

"No, I mean do I *really* know you?"

"Yes," he repeated.

"Because I feel like I *really* know you—from before."

"We've known each other for many lifetimes," said Robert while clinking the silverware into its drawer.

Martika was relieved when she heard this. It was strange to feel so intimate with someone she just met, but there was a sense of familiarity that she had felt as soon as she met Robert in the driveway.

"And what was the nature of our relationship?" asked Martika nervously. She knew whatever he said would irrevocably change her life forever, but she couldn't help herself. "Do you remember?"

"Of course I remember," Robert said plainly. "You were my mother in another life—long ago."

Tears welled up in her eyes and began to stream down her cheeks, dripping off her chin onto the bodice of her dress. Although she found it difficult to recognize this grown man as her child from a previous life, there was something deep within that reassured her that what he was saying was true.

"I'm sorry," Martika sniffled. "I don't know why I'm crying."

"I do. It's because you abandoned me when I was seven years old."

This caught Martika by surprise. "What do you mean?"

"You took your own life," Robert announced solemnly.

As soon as he said these words, a flood of terrifying images rushed into Martika's consciousness. She saw a man who she imagined was Robert's father and felt deeply how much she had loved him when they were married. The vision slowly faded into her husband on his deathbed, and she watched in sorrow as he took his last breath. When he was no longer breathing, she felt a rush of panic and was immediately overwhelmed with the responsibility of bringing up their son alone. She then witnessed several of her weakened attempts at raising Robert by herself, and began to feel consumed by her failure. She wanted to be a good mother, but the grief of losing her husband was crushing, and she didn't have the strength to care for her only child.

Hundreds of related visions flashed in succession within a matter of seconds, and Martika began to feel dizzy and nauseated from all of the information she was receiving. The images were so vivid that she could no longer discern what was real and what was imagined. But as the visions began to fade, an indelible memory was left that appeared to corroborate Robert's assertion.

"I'm sorry," she cried. "Do you forgive me?"

"No. I cannot forgive you."

"Why not?" she asked. His words felt like knives that were thrust deep into her heart.

"Forgiveness is between your soul and the universe. I can offer my love, but forgiveness isn't mine to give. That's why you keep coming back and inflicting the same lessons on yourself and your family."

What Robert was saying was hard to listen to, but there was something about it that rang true.

"Are you still having difficulty with your children?" Robert asked pointedly.

"My daughter." Martika sniffled. "She ran away from home three years ago, and I still don't know where she is." She put her head into her hands and sobbed, and her entire body began to shake. "I'm so worried about her—why is she so unhappy?"

"Because she's paying for *your* unresolved mistakes. When parents move on without working through their most significant life lessons, those lessons are passed on to their children and grandchildren until they are finally resolved. You've heard of family curses?"

Martika nodded.

"That's what a family curse is. Children are burdened with the entanglements of their parents and grandparents, and they continue to pass them down to their offspring indefinitely until the source of the entanglement has been released."

"What can I do about it?"

"I know your soul knows what to do, because you're here once again. You keep being born into the same family in order to rectify your mistakes. But then you fall back into your old patterns of feeling victimized and leave without fulfilling your *soul contract*."

"But I didn't leave my daughter; *she left me.*"

"Only after *you* left her—emotionally."

Martika was stunned by how insightful Robert was. "When did you get so smart?"

"Over the past few hundred years or so," he laughed.

"I bet your mother is very proud of you."

"I don't have a mother. I haven't had a mother since you."

Robert's cryptic words saddened Martika. Although she thought that what he was saying wasn't possible, there was an honesty in his voice that she couldn't ignore. "Why not?"

"Because I don't want one."

"How could you not want a mother?"

"You don't want me to say it."

She knew in her heart that he was right, but she couldn't help herself. It felt important to confront what he was saying—even if it would hurt her. "Yes, I do. Why?" she finally asked sheepishly.

"Because I don't want her to leave me—like *you* did."

Martika felt her breath empty from her lungs, like she had just been punched in the stomach. Within moments, another succession of visions flashed through her head. She saw her child crying out for his mother on the day she took her own life. The baby's crying echoed even louder in death than it had in life, and kept getting louder and louder. And just as she was about to let out a piercing scream to drown out the cries in her head, the visions faded to blackness . . . and within seconds she felt . . . nothing. She felt completely numb and alone, after which a profound emptiness instantly consumed her entire soul.

Martika choked on her tears while attempting to regain her grip on reality. She found herself gasping for air for several seconds until she finally calmed down. "I guess I deserved that," she whispered.

After she began breathing normally, Robert calmly asked, "What was the life you had to leave when you changed your name?"

Martika noticed the familiar way the corners of Robert's mouth turned down when he smiled and how the flat tip of his small nose reminded her of someone from her past. And the more she looked deep into his water-blue eyes, the more familiar he became, until she couldn't control her emotions anymore. Tears streamed from her eyes again, and she made no effort to wipe them as she began to speak. "My first boy," she sobbed. "I was only sixteen years old when he was born . . . and I just couldn't handle being a mother . . . I was just a child myself."

Robert instinctively covered her hand with his.

"You look like him," she said while wiping her cheek with the back of her hand. "I noticed when I first saw you earlier today, but I promised myself I wouldn't cry. I'm sorry," she sniffled. "It's not really you, is it? Are you my Donald?"

"No, I'm your Robert. But I do think you'll find your Donald very soon."

"I don't know if I can handle seeing him again," she cried. "Look at me; I'm a wreck. Before today, I didn't even remember you—no offense."

"None taken."

"But there hasn't been a single day that I didn't regret what I did to Donald. I think about him every day. I wonder where he is and what he's doing. I tried to look him up several years ago, but his father died, and I didn't know where to start. I hope he's okay." Martika's sobs returned. "I hope my baby's okay."

"I'm pretty sure he's just fine."

"I hope so," she said softly as she reorganized the seasoning bottles along the backsplash. "I'm sorry for crying—I didn't mean to break down like this."

"It's not the first time we've had this conversation," Robert said firmly. "I just hope *this* time you can find the strength to make amends to all of your children so you don't have to come back here in your next lifetime and do it all over again."

"I don't have the strength to do this again."

"Then do us all a favor and finally deal with it once and for all."

"I just don't know what to do . . ."

"You know exactly what to do. First you need to find your children, and then you need to speak from your heart. Your children don't care what's in your head; they only want your love. Share your heart with them, and never run away when they tell you what's in *their* hearts."

"Okay."

"And one more thing," said Robert.

"Yes?"

"I think you should get some allergy medicine."

CHAPTER THIRTEEN

Over the next few days, Robert and Don camped in a small tent on the far edge of Martika's property. Robert still wasn't sure how long he wanted to stay in Ashland, but as the days progressed, he began to feel there was someone important whom he was going to meet. After he announced his intention to remain in the quaint mountain town through the end of the summer, Martika arranged for him and Don to stay in a friend's traditional Native American tipi on several acres outside of town.

Although it was a long walk from the tipi to the downtown area, Robert enjoyed the exercise, and it gave Don ample time to share his feelings about

Martika. During one of the final days of springtime, Robert gathered some wood from fallen trees around the property and lit a fire in the center of the tipi.

"I guess that means we're brothers," said Don while looking into the fire.

"Hmm, I guess so," Robert laughed. "That's an interesting twist, isn't it?"

"Didn't you know we were brothers?"

"I knew you were part of my soul family, but I had no idea we had the same mother."

"What's a soul family?" Don asked.

"It's just like a normal family, but it's not limited to this lifetime. Everyone you've ever been related to, in any past life, is part of your soul family."

"That assumes you *believe* in past lives," Don said incredulously.

"You're in the body of a dog now, and you still don't believe in past lives?" Robert laughed. "Are you serious?"

"I guess not," Don sighed. "How do you know if someone is a part of your soul family?"

"It's not hard . . . you just know. There's a familiarity with members of your soul family that instantly makes you feel comfortable. You have things in common that seem very specific to you— likes and dislikes, that sort of thing. And you also have an instant connection that allows you to communicate on a deep level without having to engage in small talk like you do when you've met someone for the first time."

"That's happened to me before," said Don. "Suzanne was like that. I *hate* small talk, and she was the first person I could have a meaningful conversation with as soon as we met."

Robert nodded. "And being a Walk-in, I can tell you that time is always of the essence. Therefore, I tend to only work with members of my soul family."

After a long silence, Don said, "Robert?"

"Yes, Don."

"Does she remember me?"

"Of course she does."

"Did she recognize me? I mean, you . . . I mean, did she look at you and think of me?"

Robert laughed. "Yes, she did."

"Did she tell you why she left me? Did I do something wrong?"

"Listen, Don," said Robert, becoming very serious. "You need to let those feelings go once and for all. Not only was that at the core of your cancer, but you're preventing Mother from healing by being so selfish."

"Selfish? What do you mean?"

"You are holding on to her burden, so she's not able to deal with it."

"I don't understand."

"She was your mother, and she left you."

"I know."

"You were the baby, and she was the mother. She hurt you, and there is nothing else that matters."

"But she was such a young mother and I was so fussy. My father told me I used to cry all the time. If I'd been a happier baby, maybe she would have stayed."

"I know those are very real feelings for you, but they're simply not true."

"I don't know."

"You need to be absolutely clear about this," Robert continued. "She left you, and there was nothing you could have done about that."

"I guess so."

"And dealing with the burden of Mother leaving you is her responsibility alone. By holding on to that pain, or thinking there was something you could have done to prevent her from leaving, you have kept her burden away from her and haven't allowed her to heal herself."

"Hearing you say that makes me sad."

"That's because her burden has become a very real part of you. And you will feel a profound sense of loss when it's returned to her. But you can't replace her love with her burden. It's of no use to you, and as you know, it can cause very real damage."

"Do you think her leaving me could have caused my cancer?"

"I'm not sure. But I do know it has contributed significantly to your abandonment issues."

"How can I give it back to her?"

"I can help you with that now," said Robert. "Do you want to?"

"I guess so."

"Okay, let's begin. Repeat the following from the bottom of your heart." Robert looked deep into Don's eyes until he was convinced Don was ready, and then continued: "'Mother, you abandoned me, and that hurt me.'"

"Mother, you abandoned me"—Don paused for a moment and took a deep breath—"and that hurt me."

"Good." Robert reached into his shirt pocket and pulled out a photograph and placed it in front of Don.

"Where did you get that?!" Don exclaimed as he looked at the worn photo of his mother that he had carried in his wallet. "I thought you threw it in the river!"

"I felt it might be useful, so I removed it from your wallet before we left Eugene."

Don shook his head as he watched the fire's reflection on the photograph.

"Now, I want you to tell Mother how it made you feel when she left you."

The puppy looked up at Robert with scared eyes and began to shake. A quiet whimper escaped as the shaking became more pronounced.

"It's okay," said Robert. "I'm here, and I promise you'll be okay."

Don closed his eyes tightly and began to speak. "Mother," he said shakily, "you hurt me when you left. I didn't know where you went, and when you were gone, I felt so sad. I thought I did something wrong to make you leave. Why did you let me think that? Why did you let me think it was my fault that you left?"

Don's whole body was shaking intensely, and he struggled to take a deep breath before continuing: "I was only a baby, and I couldn't take care of myself," he whimpered. "Then you were gone. You made me feel worthless when you left—like I wasn't worthy of your love . . ."

The puppy opened his eyes and looked deep into the eyes of the photograph. "Mommy, why did you leave? I was your baby! You're not supposed to leave your baby. *Mommy, why did you leave me?!*"

Don collapsed onto the ground and began to seize. His four legs kicked independent of each other, and his entire torso shook violently. He then let out a long, throaty moan that continued for over a minute. Robert rushed to the puppy's side and caressed the back of his neck.

"It's okay," he said in a soothing voice. "You'll be okay. Just relax and take a deep breath. Let it all out and keep breathing . . ."

When Don began to calm down, his breathing returned to normal and his seizures eventually subsided.

"Good," said Robert. "You're doing great. Now there's one more thing we have to do."

The puppy let out an exhausted whimper and began shaking his head.

"It's okay," Robert continued. "We're almost done. What you need to do is repeat after me one last time: 'Mother, I'm sorry for holding on to your burden for all of these years. Your abandonment is no longer of use to me. Today, I return your burden to you so you can begin to heal.'"

When Don repeated these words, he felt a large pool of anger within him begin to dissipate. For the first time that he could remember, there was a place inside of him that was no longer filled with the emotions of his abandonment, and he instantly felt lighter. Then, almost as quickly as the anger had left, a huge flood of sadness rushed into its place, and he began to sob.

Robert let him cry for several minutes while caressing the side of his tearstained muzzle. "You know that's a hard thing to do," he said. "Dogs aren't usually able to cry."

For some reason this struck Don as funny, and he laughed out loud with a puppylike bark. "Are we done now?" he asked when his laughter subsided.

"Yes, we are, and I'm extremely proud of you. You did some very deep work, and I think you'll finally be able to move on from all of this."

"I'm really tired."

"You'll be tired while you integrate everything that happened. But there's nothing to worry about. Rest will do you good."

"Robert?"

"Yes, Don."

"Will Mother ever be able to see me?"

"I hope so," said Robert softly. "I hope so."

CHAPTER FOURTEEN

artika made her way through the tall dying grasses in the field near Dead Indian Memorial Road. After a few minutes of walking, she could see the tipi in the distance, and reflected on the many Native American ceremonies she had attended there before her friend moved to South Dakota. Native American traditions had always resonated with her, and she truly missed the tight community of the followers of that tradition. She made a mental note to ask her friend for the names of the people who had taken over hosting the ceremonies locally.

As she neared the tipi, she realized how exhausted she was. She hadn't slept very well the night before, and when she did doze off, she was disturbed by anxiety-filled dreams about her abandoned child. And for some unexplained reason, she was beginning to miss the unusual bearded man and his small black puppy who had both left her property a few days before.

Since the intense conversation with Robert the first night the two arrived, a renewed feeling of responsibility about her abandoned son had returned to her. She always felt bad about leaving him, but this time was different. Before, she had convinced herself that she had been too young—too weak to deal with her responsibility. But today, she felt proud of the fact that she had brought him into the world, and there was a very real drive to find him and make amends. And for some reason, she couldn't shake the feeling that Robert could help her locate him.

When she was standing in front of the large muslin-hued tipi, she removed an old-fashioned glass bottle of milk from her bag and absentmindedly knocked on the canvas door before realizing that it wasn't making any sound. "Knock, knock," she said aloud and waited patiently until Robert greeted her from the inside.

"Good morning," said Robert. "I had a feeling I'd see you today."

"I brought you a present," said Martika as she handed him the bottle.

"Thank you."

"It's not pasteurized," she explained. "The good bacteria and enzymes are still in there. It's the only thing that keeps my ulcer at bay, and I hear it also helps with allergies. I figured I'd better start drinking more if I want to visit this cute little thing more often."

"You're no longer allergic to dogs?"

"I took some allergy medicine just in case, but I'm hoping the milk will help over time. I can't believe such a basic food item is considered dangerous. Thank god for the 'milk smuggler,'" she laughed. "You'd think he was a drug dealer, with all the hoops you have to jump through to get one of these bottles into Oregon."

"Thanks again," smiled Robert graciously. "So what's on your mind today?"

"I can't stop dreaming about my baby." Martika felt sadness seep into the lines of her face.

"Tell me about it."

"The most intense dream I can remember is about the day I left him. It unfolded exactly as it originally happened, but when I went to his room to kiss him goodbye, you were there standing next to his bassinet."

"*I* was there?"

"Yes. It felt like you were there to protect him. And then when I bent down to kiss him goodbye, your black puppy was inside the bassinet."

"Did that worry you?"

"No, it felt right for some reason—like it was exactly the way it was supposed to be. That's what was so strange."

"Do you often dream about your baby?"

"No. I haven't dreamed about him a single time since I left him . . . I couldn't let myself go there."

"How did the dream make you feel?"

"It was surprisingly empowering—sad to confront what I had done, but by finally thinking about doing the right thing, I seem to feel better than I have in years."

"That's understandable. You've been expending huge amounts of energy to avoid dealing with your past burden, and it's been wearing you down."

"But if I wasn't dealing with it, how could I be expending energy?"

"Your soul won't let you ignore significant burdens. So if you aren't using your conscious being to deal with what you need to, your subconscious being will take over, which will begin to wear you down over time."

"I see. I'm definitely ready to deal with it now."
She was still trying to convince herself. "I probably
should find my baby and make amends. You know
what's strange? For some reason I feel your puppy
might have known him."

"It's very possible."

"What's your puppy's name again?" she asked.

"Don."

"Really?" Martika gasped. She thought that she
had imagined that. "My son was named . . ."

"I know," assured Robert.

"I wish I could talk to your puppy."

"You can," Robert replied. "Go ahead."

"Can people really talk to animals?"

"Of course they can. Although there are many
species of animals on this planet, there is only one
species of energy. And once we tune in to that
energy, we are able to communicate on a soul level
with any living being."

"Do you believe that animals have souls?"

"Of course they do. A soul is simply the energetic
embodiment of consciousness. So anything that is
alive has a soul—that's what makes it alive. Life isn't
simply a physiological by-product. The very essence
of being alive is the ability to transfer energy from
one being to another. So anything that has the

inherent ability to consciously move energy from one place to another has a soul."

"Even a plant?"

"Absolutely."

"But how do you know it's consciously transferring energy and not simply behaving mechanically in the way it was engineered?"

"I'm sure you've heard about gardens growing better when their human friends talk to them."

"Does that really work?"

"Definitely. Plants are happier when they feel loved—just like people—and happy plants grow better than sad plants. Didn't you say you studied Buddhism?"

"Yes." Martika didn't remember sharing that with Robert, but she was starting to get used to him knowing things without their having talked about them out loud.

"Then why are you having such a problem with this concept? Buddhism is very clear that all living things have a soul."

"I guess the real reason is that I couldn't bear to eat *anything* if I thought I was eating something that has a soul. Wouldn't that make me barbaric?"

"Ah yes, that *is* quite a dilemma. However, although it seems horrifying at first, many plants and animals are remarkably advanced in the spiritual practice of *service*."

"Service?"

"Yes, the concept of being in service to the universe often means being in service to another soul. And by consciously honoring that service when you're on the receiving side, you are participating in an immensely sacred ritual."

"How do I do that?"

"The easiest way is to thank them for their service and give a few moments of your time to honor their existence on this planet before you simply chew them up."

Martika cringed. "I guess that means there isn't a moral advantage to being vegetarian?"

"All living things are the same."

"Wow, I'm not sure I can handle that."

"It's okay. Do what you need to do to sustain yourself, but whenever you do eat, make sure to honor whoever is giving up their existence to benefit you."

"I'll try," said Martika.

"Okay, back to Don. Do you still want to talk to him?"

"Yes, but I don't know what to do."

"It's easy. All you have to do is *meditate outward*

and allow the space that you and Don share to fill with silence."

"I don't know what meditating outward is. I've practiced meditation for many years, but I've always been taught to go within."

"Meditating outward is a similar practice, but you also include the energy outside of yourself. Start by closing your eyes and finding the bright light within your inner world."

Martika followed Robert's instructions and inhaled a deep breath and slowly let it out. She was familiar with *this* technique of meditation, and had used it herself many times before.

"Now, move your awareness into that light until you are fully engulfed by its luminosity. Then let the light grow until it fills your entire body. Let it seep out and fill your aura that surrounds your physical body. Once you've done that, allow it to expand to include the space that is being inhabited by Don."

Martika surrendered to the white light and felt as if she was floating inside of it.

"Good. Now hold a single, simple thought in your mind, and let the answer come to you. Since you are now meditating together, you should be able to trade thoughts."

"How will I know it's not my own thought?" she asked in a quiet voice.

"Just trust the communication," Robert replied confidently. "In the same way you know that I am talking to you right now, you will know when Don talks. It's best to start out with visuals and smells if you can, since dogs have a harder time with words."

Martika remembered the gift she brought and conjured the smell of frothy unpasteurized milk. Her mouth began to water as she held the image in her mind, and right before she could imagine tasting it, a single thought appeared that there was no mistaking. Martika's heart sank.

"What's wrong?" asked Robert.

"He said he didn't want any of the milk I brought," she replied, unable to hide her disappointment.

Robert laughed.

"That's not funny!" exclaimed Martika. "Why are you laughing?"

Robert continued to laugh a deep belly laugh until he regained his composure. "Dogs are lactose intolerant," he snickered. "Of course he doesn't want any milk!"

"Oh." Martika felt embarrassed.

"Why don't you try something else? Ask him if he knows your son."

She knew that was the real reason she was here, but she wasn't sure if she was ready for that yet. She took a deep breath and filled her mind with the image of the day when she left her baby. Concentrating on his face for several minutes, she began to drift off. And as soon as she was at the point of losing consciousness, her nose filled with an unmistakable scent that she hadn't smelled in years. . . .

Hoping it would calm her baby, Martika created a unique blend of three essential oils. After mixing lavender, chamomile, and sage, she dabbed a few drops on Donald's upper lip before putting him to sleep. Ever since he was born, he constantly needed to be held, and would scream incessantly every time she put him down. But although the oils appeared to calm him for a few minutes at a time, he would quickly lose interest and return to screaming.

Martika had forgotten about that smell, and she had the unmistakable feeling that the puppy had given it to her as a gift. He seemed to know things that nobody else could know, which was simultaneously disturbing and comforting. She couldn't wrap her head around it, but she had a strong feeling that this small black puppy held a mysterious connection to her baby.

A sneeze startled Martika out of her dream state, and when she opened her eyes, she discovered that she was cradling the whimpering dog as if he was her own baby. She had subconsciously picked him up and had been gently caressing the side of his muzzle with the back of her hand. She felt self-conscious when she noticed Robert was looking at her.

"I don't think he minds." Robert smiled.

"I can't believe I left him," sniffled Martika as tears streamed down her face. "I'm a horrible person."

"Don't be so hard on yourself. Being separated from your baby was a gift from the universe."

"But it was my fault—I'm the one who left him."

"Yes, that was your role to play."

"And how is abandoning my firstborn child a *gift?*"

"The universe uses difficult situations to teach us our most significant life lessons that would be impossible to learn any other way. In your case, you need to resolve your issues with abandonment that you incurred from before."

"When I took my own life?"

"Yes. That has been your karma for many lifetimes, and every time the universe gives you a gift, you run away from it as quickly as it arrives."

"But it's painful. Why would I want to dwell on the past?"

"It's not a matter of dwelling; it's a matter of integrating. Once you allow that experience to become a part of your daily life, you will be able to draw from the wisdom that comes with it."

"I still don't understand why it's a gift."

"The *wisdom* is the gift—and the difficult experience is the carrier of that gift. But you haven't been able to accept the gift, since you've been burying that memory for so many years. Now that you're starting to integrate it into your consciousness, you can begin to draw from it and live your life with more grace."

Martika could sense her vision blurring as her eyelids began to swell. She put the sleeping puppy down on a blanket that was covered in matted black hair. "I think the allergy medicine is starting to wear off," she said after a sneeze startled the puppy awake.

"Perhaps the milk will eventually help with your allergies so you can babysit Don on occasion."

"I would like that," Martika said wistfully. "That would be nice."

After Martika left, Robert and Don remained silent for several minutes. Robert lit some sage and began smudging the ground where Martika had been, and systematically blessed the entire perimeter of the tipi while fanning the smoke outside.

"Can you believe what just happened?" Don finally broke the silence. "Wasn't that incredible?"

"Yes, thanks to *you*. By returning her burden, she is finally able to begin healing."

"Why didn't you tell her it was really me?"

"I think she was starting to figure it out."

"But why couldn't you reassure her that what she was feeling was real? So she knew that it was true?"

"If I would've told her that her son was now in the body of a dog, it would have triggered her intellect, and she probably wouldn't have been able to continue with the healing flow. Her brain would have questioned the entire experience, and she might have lost all faith in what she was feeling."

"I guess so."

"Remember, Don, this isn't just about you. She has some big issues to heal, and we've done as much as we can. The rest is up to her—just be patient. She's going to need to take some time to integrate all the soul lessons she's just learned, which are much bigger and more involved than they might have appeared. We're all subject to ancestral entanglements from our previous soul family, but in her case she's been trying to learn the same lessons for so long that many of the entanglements she needs to deal with have come from her own past lives.

"Historically, one of her tools of avoidance has been to give herself completely to her children once she's been confronted with what she has done to them. This allows her to begin to live *their* lives so she can once again avoid living her own. That's why your situation is so perfect. Today she was forced to confront abandoning you, but because of your current form, she was unable to begin living your life.

"Over the next few months she'll have the opportunity to integrate all of this information while unraveling her entanglements. What she did to you is her biggest burden of this lifetime. And by you being near her without being in human form, it allows her to confront that burden without using it as an excuse to lose herself in it.

"Hopefully soon she'll be able to take responsibility for what she has done to each of us, while being honest about what she has done to herself. I've been waiting for this day much longer than you have, and I pray that this time she'll finally be able to release us from all of her karmic responsibilities."

CHAPTER FIFTEEN

"Why did he come *here?*" Suzanne asked aloud as she walked across the parking lot toward the bright yellow caution tape. The warm air was remarkably calm in Hellgate Canyon, yet scattered on the ground were broken shards of glass and red reflector plastic that hinted at the tragedy that took place before.

When she reached the wall that had been unsuccessful in preventing her husband's car from plunging down the ravine, she noticed a collection of medium-sized river rocks that had become dislodged from the wall's mortar when Don's car had apparently rammed through it. She couldn't believe such a flimsy barrier was expected to ensure safety on such an obviously dangerous road, and she could feel her anger return once again. "So pointless," she fumed while shaking her head. "How could this have happened?"

At the base of the ravine, she saw a bright emerald pool cradled by sheer granite cliffs. The beauty of the steep canyon was undeniable, somehow enhanced by the thousands of razor-sharp stones flowing toward the water in an enormous granite waterfall that was easily twenty stories high.

Suzanne had been wondering if she should give Don a memorial service, but she wasn't sure who should be invited. She didn't think that anyone would show up except for his slimy lawyer friend— and she didn't want to be alone with *him,* no matter what the occasion. But the real reason she didn't want a memorial was because she didn't think that Don deserved it. She was still angry at him for leaving her so suddenly. If he was really in that much pain, she would have understood—but they were a team; he had no right to make *that* decision on his own.

Without thinking, she straddled the wall and quickly found a path that meandered along the precarious rock face. After just a few steps, she slipped on a rock and lost her footing, falling backward and sliding down the steep embankment in a blinding cloud of dust. Fortunately, she was able to grab on to a thin oak branch, which prevented her from tumbling to the bottom. Suzanne's heart raced as she gripped the branch with both hands and held on tightly while catching her breath.

After several minutes of struggling, she pulled herself up with the surprisingly sturdy oak branch and resolved to find a pathway down to the water. When her eyes were able to adjust to the glare of the bright sunlight, she saw a narrow footpath worn into the straw-colored grasses that had grown in between the cracks of the large boulders.

Walking just a few minutes, she came to a dead end at the edge of the steep cliff. She retraced her steps and followed a second fork along the back side of the canyon. The path circuitously wandered along the rock face before once again ending at the edge of another steep cliff.

Lying down on her stomach, Suzanne inched slowly along the ledge that cantilevered out from the mountain's face—high above the glimmering green pool below. When she reached the edge of the rock, she shakily tried to maintain her balance without the benefit of anything to hold on to. After successfully standing upright, she briefly looked down to the water and nearly passed out from the vertigo. Closing her eyes tightly, she instinctively outstretched her arms in a T shape in order to stay balanced.

In that moment an overwhelming urge came over her to jump off the cliff and join Don in the water below. She wanted to know what her husband had felt was more compelling than being alive with his wife. The emerald pool was Don's mistress, and Suzanne became obsessed with confronting her charms.

With her eyes still closed, Suzanne stood on the precarious boulder for several minutes as she tried to decide what to do next. Beads of sweat gathered on the bridge of her nose, and her throat started to constrict. The temperature gauge in her car had said it was ninety-seven degrees outside when she arrived, but she hadn't realized how warm it really was until she was standing on the cliff without the benefit of shade.

She began to feel light-headed, and her vision pulsed to darkness every few seconds as the heat seeped into her every pore. A gentle breeze caressed her cheek, and subconsciously a smile crept onto her lips as she remembered something from her childhood: *"Listen to the words that the wind carries,"* her grandfather would say. *"They are the only words that can be trusted."*

Suzanne hadn't listened to the wind since she was a little girl, but remembered that it always seemed to tell her what she needed to hear. She hoped that she could remember how to do it and tried to clear her brain of all the distracting thoughts that kept it occupied. Once her mind was quiet, she began to listen to what the wind had to say.

At first she couldn't hear anything, but after a few minutes, she was able to discern the distinct sounds that the winds were carrying. She heard the sound of a bird above her, and the leaves rustling in the trees. The trickling sounds from the river below were carried up the canyon walls, and she was eventually enveloped by the calming echoes of water. After several minutes, she was finally able to stop *hearing* the wind, and began to *listen*. Slowly, words emerged that were as familiar as they were unknown:

scoʈʈ blum

Harbinger, home within
Surrender to the mystery
One of three, we all become
Rain, tree, crow.

She'd never heard that poem before and wasn't sure what it meant, but for some reason it comforted her. It provided a sense of calm and appeared to contain a profound wisdom that couldn't be explained. Whispering the poem several times in hushed tones, she felt herself rise above the rock face as if she was gently being lifted by the warm breeze. She couldn't feel her feet anymore—nor, for that matter, her ankles or calves. It was as if she had begun to levitate and was gently floating above the canyon.

Instinctively, she held her breath for several seconds, and when she opened her eyes, she saw the sun dancing with the clouds in the sky above. A single sunbeam appeared to fall from the clouds, and as she followed its luminosity to the river below, she thought she saw the unmistakable outline of Don's car underneath the water. The police had said they were going to remove it, but perhaps they hadn't been able to yet.

Suzanne didn't want to look down to her feet, but she knew she had to. As soon as she saw that they were still firmly planted on the ground, she couldn't keep herself from being disappointed. The floating feeling began to dissipate, and the words of the poem drifted away as the breeze suddenly stopped.

"I can make it to the water if I jump out far enough," she said aloud, trying to convince herself. She then carefully bent down and picked up a small pebble that had lodged itself within a crack in the boulder she was standing on. With as much force as she could muster, she threw the stone as far as she could. It flew effortlessly a few hundred feet before gracefully descending toward the emerald pool. Her heart sank when it failed to reach the water and instead plummeted into the rocks at least fifty yards from the riverbank.

Suzanne closed her eyes tightly and tried to summon the floating feeling that she had felt before, but she wasn't able to. Her feet felt more firmly planted on the ground than they had in years. It was as if the weight had returned to her legs after they'd been hollow for as long as she could remember. It was a reassuring feeling; however, it wasn't what she wanted now—she wanted to float through the sky and into the water.

She tried to recall the enigmatic poem that the wind had carried, but she had already forgotten the words. *Something about a bird,* she thought, *or maybe a flower?* The wind remained still, and she began to lose hope when she finally acknowledged the obvious: "I don't think I can make it to the water from here," she whispered softly as tears began streaming down her cheek. "Maybe I can get in somewhere upstream."

Without warning, the wind gusted with such intense force that Suzanne was nearly knocked off balance. And deep within the loud rumbling sounds of the gust, she heard the wind's unmistakable voice once again:

He can't be followed.

The wind continued to gust for several seconds, and then it fell completely still, leaving a deafening silence in its wake.

"Why can't I come?" Suzanne screamed at the top of her lungs, and the canyon echoed her plea. "Why can't I be with him anymore?" she cried in desperate resignation, and began to shake uncontrollably as tears fell from her eyes to her lips. As the last shred of hope escaped into the void of the very canyon that took her husband, Suzanne suddenly felt more alone than she ever had before.

Don was her entire world, and he was gone. Her husband had left her, and he was never coming back.

Then the heavy feeling in her legs started to rise and fill the rest of her body. It seeped into her belly and throughout her torso—then into her arms, her neck, and finally her head. She felt unusually solid and stable in her footing, and her loneliness began to evolve into a profound sense of independence. Without kneeling down, she calmly turned around and assuredly scaled the boulder back to the footpath. She knew Hellgate Canyon was no longer her place to be, and she suddenly felt as if it was time to leave.

Suzanne deliberately walked back to her car without turning around. "I would have followed him anywhere," she whispered solemnly as she wiped the remaining tears from her cheek, "but I guess I can't do that anymore."

CHAPTER SIXTEEN

After fully exploring the town, Robert and Don began to frequent the Co-op, which appeared to be *the* meeting place for all the locals. Every morning Robert would carry the puppy from the tipi to the natural-food store when it opened at 7 A.M. He would sit in meditation opposite the glass doors of the exit and tune in to the energy of everyone who was leaving with their groceries. As they entered the store, their energy was very chaotic, but when exiting, the patrons were much more at ease and often had a singular focus.

Most of the time their thoughts were quite mundane, like: *I have to get back to work,* or *I'm so tired today.* But more often than he would have expected, someone would have a thought that Robert would find intriguing, such as: *You can't get clean in dirty water.* Robert began to write these thoughts down on used cardboard panels that the Co-op was recycling, and then he would share these profundities with everyone who exited the store.

Often, people would glance at the signs and walk by without saying anything, but occasionally a particular sign would hit a nerve. On an exceptionally beautiful day at the beginning of summer, he transcribed a thought from a silver-haired lady with kind green eyes:

Always receive with grace.

For some reason, this particular sign encouraged a larger number of shoppers than normal to share their money with him. It didn't occur to Robert that people would pay him to give a voice to other people's thoughts, but he was thankful, since it made taking care of Don and himself much easier.

"Today is the first day of summer," said Robert while repositioning his sign.

"Honey Moon," added Don.

"Aw, you remembered." Robert smiled. "Happy honeymoon to you, too."

"The days will be getting shorter."

"It's also the warmest time of the year."

Don closed his eyes at the moment that a boyish young man with shaggy brown hair walked out the Co-op doors. He was dressed inconspicuously in jeans and a T-shirt, but there was something about his energy that attracted Robert's attention.

As the young man exited the double doors, Robert noticed him reading the sign intently.

"That's ironic," the young man said.

"What's ironic?" asked Robert.

He kept walking past, and Robert repeated, "What's ironic?"

The young man slowly turned around and with a startled look on his face, said, "It's ironic that you're giving advice on how to receive, when you're asking for money."

"I'm not asking for anything." Robert smirked. "Right now I'm giving."

"So when are you going to give *me* something?"

"I already have, but you wouldn't accept it in the manner it was offered."

"Oh, I think you're mistaken. You definitely haven't given me anything. Perhaps you confused me with someone else."

"No, I didn't confuse you with anyone else!" Robert tried to act annoyed for effect. "Please leave now; I'm very busy."

The young man looked around at the unusually empty parking lot, obviously very confused.

"Please leave now," Robert repeated and turned away. The young man stood stunned for a second before walking away from the Co-op.

"That was mean," said Don. "Why did you mess with him like that?"

"To make an impression," answered Robert.

"Well, I think you did *that*. And what was all that about *giving him something?*"

"He'll find out soon enough," laughed Robert. "It's already been set into motion—he'll be back to find out more."

At that moment a young mother exited the Co-op, balancing a bag of groceries while pushing a baby stroller. Robert wrote down her thought, which seemed to follow the previous sign perfectly.

I want an orange.
What do you want?

Within ten minutes, Robert had acquired nearly a dozen oranges. He put the citrus into his drawstring bag for later and patiently awaited the young man's return. After nearly an hour, Robert saw him enter the store once again after glancing in their direction.

"See, I told you he'd be back," said Robert. "I'll bet you ten oranges to one he's going to give us another navel."

"I hate oranges," said Don. "I can't even stand the *thought* of fruit anymore."

Within just a few minutes, the young man exited the glass double doors and tossed an orange to Robert.

"Thanks," said Robert while trying to muster a look of surprise and gratefulness. "That's the best thing that's happened to me all day."

"So you can help me get what I want?"

"Of course I can," replied Robert.

"How can you do that?"

"You can manifest anything you want."

"Oh, really? Why don't *you* do it?"

"I do, every day."

"Then why are you still homeless?"

"Why do you think I'm homeless?" Robert wanted to make a point about not making any assumptions. It would be an important lesson if they began to do any work together.

"What do you manifest?" the young man asked after a long pause.

"Today I manifested an orange."

He laughed. "All you did was write a sign that said you wanted an orange."

"And you gave me one. So clearly I was successful at manifesting." Robert smiled proudly.

"So if I want a million dollars, all I have to do is make a sign that says 'Give me a million dollars' and someone will just give it to me?"

"Do you believe that will happen?"

"Of course not! There's no way some guy is going to see a sign and give me a million bucks!"

"Then you answered your own question."

"So you agree—you can't just make anything you want appear out of nowhere."

"No. I simply agree *you* don't believe that's the right way to manifest a million dollars. Manifesting isn't about making a halfhearted effort and then failing. Manifesting is about aligning your goals and your destiny so they become one. You have to believe without a doubt and act without pause, or else you're wasting your time. Do you really want a million dollars?"

"Of course I do."

"I don't believe you."

"Why not?"

"Because I have an orange, and it doesn't look like you have anywhere near a million dollars in your pocket. What do you *really* want?" Robert asked.

"To be happy," the young man answered after a long pause.

"Now that's something I can help you with. Once you're honest with yourself, you're halfway there. I'm Robert," he said with his hand outstretched.

"I'm Scott." They shook hands.

"Nice to meet you, Scott. And this is my puppy, Don. Come back here tomorrow around the same time, and I'll have something for you."

Scott walked up the hill toward town with his groceries.

"I told you I made an impression on him," Robert said to the sleeping puppy.

At that instant, a bright blue dragonfly descended from the trees above and hovered three inches from Robert's nose. He looked deep into the dragonfly's eyes and nodded slowly. "Yes, that was definitely him," Robert said aloud. "And now the fun begins."

AFTERWORD

I sincerely hope you have enjoyed reading about Robert and Don's adventures during the first part of their time together. If you're interested in what happens next, the journey continues in *Waiting for Autumn*, which is available at your local bookstore or on my website at: **www.scottblum.net**. Here's a little bit about *Waiting for Autumn:*

"<u>Waiting for Autumn</u> is a warm and revealing book about personal transformation. Its narrative reveals the honesty of one who has really walked the path of forgiveness and divine connection and found the rewards of intuition, mission, and synchronistic flow. This book will speak to everyone."

— **James Redfield,** the author of
The Celestine Prophecy

Until we meet again, I wish you the best on your personal journey and hope that you will always be aware enough to follow your own destiny.

— Scott Blum
Ashland, Oregon

ABOUT THE AUTHOR

Scott Blum is the best-selling author of *Waiting for Autumn* and the co-founder of the popular inspirational website DailyOM (**dailyom.com**). He is also a successful multimedia artist who has collaborated with several popular authors, musicians, and visual artists and has produced many critically acclaimed works, including a series featuring ancient meditation music from around the world. Scott lives in the mountains of Ashland, Oregon, with Madisyn Taylor—his wife, business partner, and soul mate.

For more about Scott Blum and his projects, visit: **www.scottblum.net**.

RESOURCES

DailyOM is the online resource that Scott Blum and his wife, Madisyn Taylor, run together. It has become the premier destination for providing inspirational content, products, and courses around the globe from some of today's best-selling authors and luminaries.

"Inspirational thoughts for a happy,
healthy and fulfilling day."

www.dailyom.com

Judith Blackstone is an amazing teacher and creator of Realization Process, which encompasses many ideas, including her profound work with embodiment.

"For spiritual realization to be an actual trans-formation of our being, rather than just a change in our beliefs, it requires an awakening of fundamental consciousness in the whole body."

www.realizationcenter.com

Hay House Titles of Related Interest

YOU CAN HEAL YOUR LIFE, the movie,
starring Louise L. Hay & Friends
(available as a 1-DVD program and an expanded 2-DVD set)
Watch the trailer at: **www.LouiseHayMovie.com**

THE SHIFT, the movie,
starring Dr. Wayne W. Dyer
(available as a 1-DVD program and an expanded 2-DVD set)
Watch the trailer at: **www.DyerMovie.com**

*DAILYOM: **Learning to Live,*** by Madisyn Taylor

***LINDEN'S LAST LIFE: The Point of No Return
Is Just the Beginning,*** by Alan Cohen

***MESSAGES FROM SPIRIT: The Extraordinary Power of
Oracles, Omens, and Signs,*** by Colette Baron-Reid

REPETITION: Past Lives, Life, and Rebirth,
by Doris E. Cohen, Ph.D.

SOLOMON'S ANGELS, by Doreen Virtue

***VISIONSEEKER: Shared Wisdom from the
Place of Refuge,*** by Hank Wesselman, Ph.D.

All of the above are available at your local bookstore,
or may be ordered by contacting Hay House (see next page).

We hope you enjoyed this Hay House book. If you'd like to receive our online catalog featuring additional information on Hay House books and products, or if you'd like to find out more about the Hay Foundation, please contact:

Hay House, Inc., P.O. Box 5100, Carlsbad, CA 92018-5100

(760) 431-7695 or **(800) 654-5126**
(760) 431-6948 (fax) or **(800) 650-5115 (fax)**
www.hayhouse.com® • **www.hayfoundation.org**

Published and distributed in Australia by: Hay House Australia Pty. Ltd., 18/36 Ralph St., Alexandria NSW 2015
Phone: 612-9669-4299 • *Fax:* 612-9669-4144
www.hayhouse.com.au

Published and distributed in the United Kingdom by: Hay House UK, Ltd., 292B Kensal Rd., London W10 5BE
Phone: 44-20-8962-1230 • *Fax:* 44-20-8962-1239
www.hayhouse.co.uk

Published and distributed in the Republic of South Africa by: Hay House SA (Pty), Ltd., P.O. Box 990, Witkoppen 2068
Phone/Fax: 27-11-467-8904 • info@hayhouse.co.za
www.hayhouse.co.za

Published in India by: Hay House Publishers India, Muskaan Complex, Plot No. 3, B-2, Vasant Kunj, New Delhi 110 070
Phone: 91-11-4176-1620 • *Fax:* 91-11-4176-1630
www.hayhouse.co.in

Distributed in Canada by: Raincoast, 9050 Shaughnessy St., Vancouver, B.C. V6P 6E5 • *Phone:* (604) 323-7100
Fax: (604) 323-2600 • www.raincoast.com

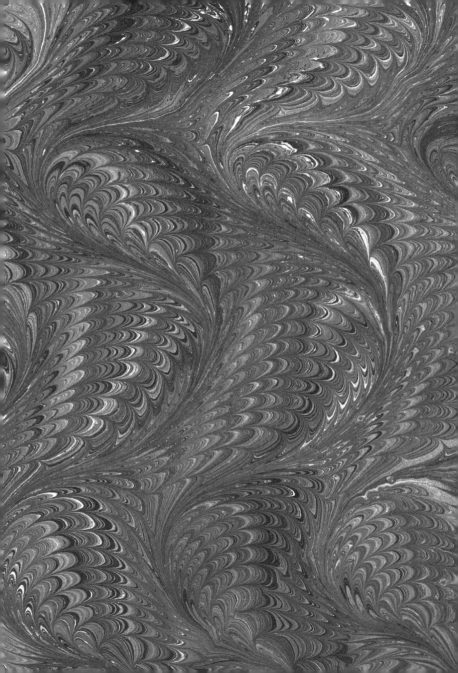

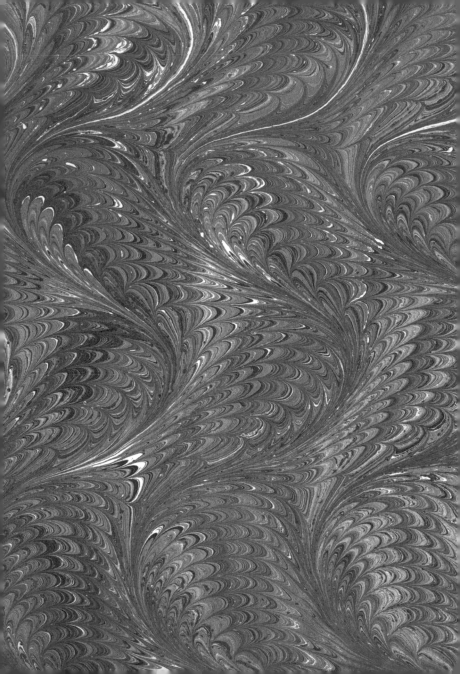